HANS CHRISTIAN ANDERSEN
FAIRY TALES

HANS CHRISTIAN ANDERSEN
FAIRY TALES

Illustrated by Svend Otto S.

Translated by R.P. Keigwin

Gyldendal

Hans Christian Andersen Fairy Tales
Illustrated by Svend Otto S
Translation copyright © 1976 Hans Reitzels Forlag Denmark
This edition: © Gyldendal 2003
Illustrations copyright © Svend Otto S.
1975, 1989, 1992, 1993, 1995, 1996
This Book has been typeset in Garamond by Viborg Maskinsætteri
and printed by Nørhaven Book, Viborg
Printed in Denmark 2003
ISBN 87-02-01984-1

CONTENTS

THE PRINCESS AND THE PEA

Once upon a time there was a Prince, who wanted to have a Princess of his own, but she must be a proper Princess. So he travelled all over the world in order to find such a one, but every time there was something wrong. There were plenty of Princesses, but he could never quite make out if they were real Princesses; there was always something that wasn't quite right. So he came back home and was very much upset, because he did so long for a real Princess.

One evening a terrible storm blew up. There was lightning and thunder, the rain came pouring down – it was something dreadful! All at once there was a knock at the city gate, and the old King went out to open it.

It was a Princess standing outside. But goodness! what a sight she was with the rain and the weather! The water was running all down her hair and her clothes, and in at the tip of her shoes and out again at the heels; and yet she declared she was a real Princess.

"Well, we shall soon see about that!" thought the old Queen. She didn't say anything, but she went into the bedroom, took off all the bedclothes and placed a pea on the bottom of the bed; then she took twenty mattresses and laid them on top of the pea, and then again twenty of the softest featherbeds on top of the mattresses. That's where the Princess had to sleep for the night.

In the morning they asked her how she had slept. "Oh, dreadfully badly!" said the Princess. "I hardly had a wink of sleep all night! Goodness knows what there was in the bed! I was lying on something so hard that I'm simply black and blue all over. It's perfectly dreadful!"

So then of course they could see that she really was a Princess, because she had felt the pea right through the twenty mattresses and the twenty feather-beds. Nobody but a real Princess could have such a tender skin as that.

And so the Prince took her to wife, because now he knew that he had a proper Princess. And the pea was sent to the museum, where it is still to be seen, unless someone has taken it.

There, that's something like a story, isn't it?

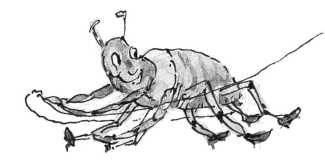

THUMBELINA

$\mathcal{T}$here once was a woman who did so want to have a wee child of her own, but she had no idea where she was to get it from. So she went off to an old witch and said to her, "I would so dearly like to have a little child. Do please tell me where I can find one."

"Oh, that!" said the witch, "Nothing easier. Take this barleycorn – mind you, it's not the kind that grows out in the fields or that the fowls are fed with. Put it in a flower-pot, and see what happens!"

"Thank you very much", said the woman, giving the witch a shilling. She went straight home and planted the barleycorn, and in no time there came up a lovely great flower which looked just like a tulip, only the petals were shut tight as though it were still in bud.

"It *is* a pretty flower," said the woman, and she gave the lovely red and yellow petals a kiss; but directly she kissed it, the flower burst open with a pop. It was a real tulip – that was plain enough now – but, sitting on the green pistil in the middle of the flower, was a tiny little girl. She was delicately pretty and no taller than your thumb, so she was given the name of Thumbelina.

A nicely varnished walnut-shell did for her cradle, blue violet petals for her mattress, and a rose-leaf for her counterpane. That was where she slept at night; but in the daytime she played about on the table, where the woman had put a plate with a wreath of flowers. These dipped

their stalks down into the water, in the middle of which floated a large tulip petal where Thumbelina could sit and row herself from one side of the plate to the other, using a couple of white horsehairs as oars. It was a most charming sight. She could sing, too; in the sweetest little voice you ever heard.

One night, as she lay in her pretty bed, a hideous toad came hopping in through a broken pane in the window. It was a great ugly slimy toad, and it jumped straight down on to the table where Thumbelina was lying asleep under her red rose-leaf.

"She would make a nice wife for my son," thought the toad, and she snatched up the walnut-shell in which Thumbelina was sleeping and hopped off with her through the window into the garden.

There was a wide brook running through it, but the bank was swampy and muddy, and here the toad lived with her son. Ugh! wasn't he ugly and horrible – just like his mother! "Koax, koax, brekke-ke-kex" was all he could say, when he saw the pretty little girl in the walnut-shell.

"Sh! Not so loud, or you'll wake her," said the old toad. "She might yet run away from us, for she's as light as swan's-down. Let's put her out in the brook on one of those broad water-

lilies. She's so small and light that its leaf will be like an island for her. She can't escape from there, and in the meantime we'll get the best room ready under the mud for you two to live in."

There were quite a lot of water-lilies growing on the water with their broad green leaves which seem to be floating on the surface. The biggest of them all happened to be the furthest away, but the old toad swam out and placed the walnut-shell on it with Thumbelina still sleeping inside.

Early the next morning the poor little thing woke up and, when she saw where she was, she began to cry bitterly, for the big green leaf had water all round it and she couldn't possibly reach the bank.

The old toad stayed down in the mud and decorated her room with rushes and yellow water-lilies, so as to make everything quite snug for her new daughter-in-law. Then she swam out with her son to the waterlily where Thumbelina was standing, for they wanted to fetch that fine walnut bed and put it up in the bridal-chamber before she came herself. The old toad made a low curtsey to her in the water and said, "Here's my son – he's to be your husband. You'll have a lovely home together down in the mud."

"Koax, koax, brekke-ke-kex!" was all that the son could say.

Then they took the pretty little bed and swam away with it. But Thumbelina sat all alone on the green leaf and cried, for she didn't want to live with the horrible toad or to marry her ugly son. The little fishes, swimming down there in the water, had caught sight of the toad and heard what she said. So they poked their heads out of the water; they were so anxious to have a look at the little girl. Directly they saw her, they found her charming, and they couldn't bear to think that she must go and live with the ugly toad. No, that must never happen! They all swarmed together down in the water round the green stalk that held the leaf she was standing on and gnawed it through with their teeth; whereupon the leaf floated away with Thumbelina down the brook, far away where the toad could never reach her.

Thumbelina went sailing past all sorts of places, and the little birds perched in the bushes saw her and trilled out, "What a pretty little lady!" The leaf that carried her floated further and further on; and thus it was that Thumbelina began her journey abroad.

A dainty little white butterfly kept on fluttering round and round her, till at last it settled on the leaf, for it had taken a great liking to Thumbelina; and she too was pleased, because the toad couldn't reach her now and she was sailing through such a lovely part of the brook. The sunshine gleamed on the water like the finest gold. Then she took her sash and tied one end of it round the butterfly, while the other end she made fast to the leaf; and this at once gathered speed – and so did Thumbelina because, you see, she was standing on the leaf. Just then a large cockchafer came flying up and, catching sight of her, clutched her round her slender waist and flew with her up into a tree. But the green leaf went floating on and the butterfly with it, because it had been tied to the leaf and couldn't manage to free itself.

Gracious, what a fright it gave poor Thumbelina, when the cockchafer flew up into the tree with her! Still, what upset her even more was the thought of the pretty white butterfly that she had tied to the leaf; for unless it could manage to free itself, it would certainly starve to death. But that didn't worry the cockchafer in the slightest. He settled beside her on the largest green leaf in the tree, gave her some nectar from the blossoms and said how pretty she was, although she wasn't a bit like a cockchafer. Later on, all the other cockchafers living in the tree came to call on her. They stared at Thumbelina, and the young lady cockchafers shrugged their feelers – "Why, she's only got two legs," they said. "What a pitiable sight!" "She hasn't any feelers," they went on. "She's so pinched in at the waist – ugh! she might almost be a human. Isn't she ugly!" exclaimed all the lady cockchafers. And yet Thumbelina was really so pretty. And that's what the cockchafer thought who had carried her off; but when all the others kept saying how

ugly she was, then at length he thought so too and would have nothing to do with her; she could go where she liked. They flew with her down from the tree and sat her on a daisy. There she cried and cried, because she was so ugly that the cockchafers wouldn't have her; and all the time she was as beautiful as can be – as exquisite as the loveliest rose-petal.

Right through the summer poor Thumbelina lived quite alone in that enormous wood. She took blades of grass and plaited herself a bed, which she hung under a large dock-leaf, so as to be out of the rain. She got her food from the honey in the flowers, and her drink from the morning dew on the leaves; and in this way summer and autumn went by. But now came winter – the long, cold winter. All the birds that had sung to her so beautifully now flew away;

the trees and flowers withered; the great dockleaf she had been living under furled itself into nothing but a faded yellow stalk. She felt the cold most terribly, for her clothes were by this time in tatters, and she herself was so tiny and delicate, poor Thumbelina, that she would surely be frozen to death. It began snowing, and every snowflake that fell on her was like a whole shovelful being thrown on us, for we are quite big and she was no taller than your thumb. So she wrapped herself up in a dead leaf, but there was no warmth in that, and she shivered with cold.

On the fringe of the wood where she had now come to was a large cornfield; but the corn

had long been harvested, and only the bare barren stubble thrust up from the frozen earth. It was just like an entire forest for her to walk through – oh, and she was shivering with cold! At length she came to the field-mouse's door. It was a little hole down below the stubble. There the field-mouse had a fine snug place to live in, with a whole roomful of corn and a splendid kitchen and dining-room. Poor Thumbelina stood just inside the door like any other wretched beggar-girl and asked for a little bit of barleycorn, for she hadn't had a scrap to eat for two days.

"You poor mite!" said the field-mouse, for at heart she was a kind old thing. "Come you in and have a bite with me in my warm room."

As she at once took a liking to Thumbelina she made a suggestion. "You're quite welcome to stay with me for the winter," she said, "as long as you'll keep my rooms nice and tidy and also tell me stories, for I'm so fond of stories." And Thumbelina did what the kind old field-mouse asked for and was extremely comfortable there.

"I dare say we shall have a visitor before long," said the field-mouse. "My neighbour generally pays me a call once a week. His house is even snugger than mine, with goodsized rooms, and he wears such a lovely black velvet coat. If only you could get him for a husband, you'd be comfortably off. But his sight's very bad. You must tell him all the nicest stories you know."

Thumbelina took no notice of all this; she had no intention of marrying the neighbour, for he was a mole. He came and called in his black velvet coat. He was so rich and clever, according

to the field-mouse, and his home was twenty times the size of the field-mouse's. He was very learned, but he couldn't bear sunshine and pretty flowers; he said all sorts of nasty things about them, never having seen them. Thumbelina had to sing, and she sang both "Ladybird, ladybird, fly away home" and "Ring-a-ring-o'roses"; and the mole fell in love with her because of her pretty voice, but he didn't say anything – he was much too cautious a man for that.

He had lately dug a long passage for himself through the earth, leading from his house to theirs. Here the field-mouse and Thumbelina were invited to stroll whenever they cared to. But he told them not to be afraid of the dead bird lying in the passage; it was a whole bird with beak and feathers, that had evidently only just died as the winter began and was now buried in the very spot where he had made his underground passage.

The mole took a bit of touchwood in his mouth – for in the dark that shines just like fire – and went ahead to give them a light in the long dark passage. When they came to where the dead bird was lying, the mole tilted his broad snout up to the ceiling and thrust through the earth; making a large hole through which the light could penetrate. In the middle of the floor lay a dead swallow with its pretty wings folded close in to its sides, and head and legs tucked in beneath its feathers. The poor bird must have died of cold. Thumbelina felt so sorry for it; she was very fond of all the little birds that had sung and twittered for her so sweetly right through the summer. But the mole kicked at it with his stumpy legs, saying, "That won't chirp any more! How wretched it must be to be born a little bird! Thank goodness no child of mine ever will be. A bird like that has of course nothing but its twitter and is bound to starve to death when winter comes."

"Just what I'd expect to hear from a sensible man like you," said the field-mouse. "What has a bud to show for all its twittering, when winter comes? It must starve and freeze. But I suppose that's considered a great thing."

Thumbelina didn't say a word, but when the other two turned their back on the bird, she stooped down and, smoothing aside the feathers that lay over its head, she kissed its closed eyes. "Who knows – this may be the very one," she thought, "that used to sing so beautifully to me last summer."

The mole now filled in the hole where the daylight shone through and saw the two ladies home. But that night Thumbelina simply couldn't sleep; so she got up, and plaited a fine big blanket of hay, which she carried down and spread all over the dead bird, and she took some soft cotton-wool she had found in the field-mouse's room and tucked this in at the sides, so that the bird might lie warm in the cold earth.

"Goodbye, you lovely little bird," she said. "Goodbye, and thank you for your beautiful singing last summer, when all the trees were green and the sun was so bright and warm." Then she laid her head up against the bird's breast – but at the same moment she got such a fright, for she heard a kind of thumping inside. It was the bird's heart. The bird wasn't dead; it had been lying numb and unconscious and now, as it grew warm again, it revived.

You see, in autumn the swallows all fly away to the warm countries, but if there's one that lags behind it gets so cold that it falls down dead. There it lies, where it fell, and the cold snow covers it over.

Thumbelina was all of a tremble from the fright she had, for the bird was of course an immense great creature beside her, who was no taller than your thumb. However, she took courage and tucked the cottonwool still more closely round the poor swallow and fetched a curled mint leaf that she had been using herself for a counterpane and spread this over the bird's head.

The following night she again stole down to the bird, and this time it had quite revived; but it was so feeble that it could only open its eyes for a short moment to look at Thumbelina, standing there with a bit of touchwood in her hand, for she had no other light.

"Thank you, my darling child," said the sick swallow. "I'm lovely and warm now. I shall soon get back my strength and be able to fly again, out in the warm sunshine."

"Ah, but it's so cold out of doors," she said. "It's snowing and freezing. Stay in your warm bed; I'll look after you all right."

Then she brought the swallow some water, in the petal of a flower, and the bird drank it and told her how it had torn one of its wings on a bramble and therefore couldn't fly as fast as the other swallows when they flew far, far away to the warm countries. At last it had fallen to the ground, but it couldn't remember anything after that and had no idea how it came to be where it was.

The swallow now remained here all through the winter, and Thumbelina took care of it and grew very fond of it. Neither the mole nor the field-mouse heard anything at all about this; they had no liking for the poor wretched swallow.

As soon as spring had arrived and the sun had begun to warm the earth, the swallow said goodbye to Thumbelina, who opened up the hole that the mole had made in the roof of the passage. The sun came shining in so pleasantly, and the swallow asked if she would like to come too; she could sit on its back, and they would fly far out into the green forest. But Thumbelina knew that it would grieve the old field-mouse, if she left her like that.

"No, I can't," said Thumbelina. "Goodbye goodbye, you dear kind girl," said the swallow, as it flew into the open sunshine. Thumbelina gazed after it with tears in her eyes, for she was so fond of the poor swallow.

"Tweet-tweet!" sang the bird and flew off into the woods …

Thumbelina felt so sad. She was never allowed to go out into the warm sunshine. The corn that had been sown in the field above the fieldmouse's home was certainly very tall; so that it was like a dense wood for the poor little girl, who after all was only an inch high.

"You will have to start making your wedding trousseau this summer," the field-mouse told her, because by now their neighbour, the tiresome tedious mole in the black velvet coat, had proposed to her. "You'll need to have both woollens and linen – something for every occasion – when you're married to the mole."

So Thumbelina had to spin from a distaff, and the field-mouse engaged four spiders to spin and weave day and night. Every evening there was a visit from the mole, who always kept on about how, when summer was over, the sun wasn't nearly so warm, whereas now it scorched the earth till it was as hard as a stone. Yes, and when the summer had ended there was to be his wedding with Thumbelina. But she wasn't at all pleased, for she found the mole such a terrible bore. Every morning, as the sun rose, and every evening as it set, she stole out to the door, and when the wind parted the ears of corn so that she could see the blue sky, she thought how lovely and bright it was out there and did so wish she could catch sight of the dear swallow once more; but the bird never came again and had evidently flown far off into the beautiful green forest.

Now it was autumn, and Thumbelina had the whole of her trousseau ready.

"Your wedding will be in four weeks' time," the field-mouse told her. But Thumbelina wept and said she wouldn't marry the tedious mole.

"Hoity-toity!" said the field-mouse. "Don't you be so pig-headed, or I'll bite you with my white teeth. Why, he's a splendid husband for you. The Queen herself hasn't anything like his black velvet coat. His kitchen and cellar are both of the best. You ought to thank Heaven he's yours."

The wedding-day arrived. The mole was already there to fetch Thumbelina. She would have to live with him deep down under the earth and never come out into the warm sunshine, for he didn't care for that. The poor child was very sad at having to say goodbye to the beautiful sun, which she had at least been allowed to look at from the doorway when she was living with the field-mouse.

"Goodbye, bright sun!" she said and, stretching out her arms to it, she also took a few steps out from the field-mouse's dwelling; for the harvest was in, and nothing was left but the dry stubble. "Goodbye, goodbye," she said, throwing her tiny arms round a little red flower standing near. "Remember me to the dear swallow, if you happen to see it."

"Tweet-tweet!" she heard suddenly over her head. She looked up, and there was the swallow just passing. How delighted it was to see Thumbelina! She told the bird how she disliked having to marry the ugly mole and to live deep down under the earth where the sun never shone. She couldn't help crying at the thought.

"The cold winter will soon be here," said the swallow. "I'm going far away to the warm countries. Will you come with me? You can sit on my back. Just tie yourself on with your sash, and away we'll fly from the ugly mole and his dingy house, far away across the mountains, to the warm countries, where the sun shines more brightly than it does here and there's always summer with its lovely flowers. Dear little Thumbelina, do come with me – you who saved my life when I lay frozen stiff in that dismal cellar."

"Yes, I'll come with you," said Thumbelina. She climbed on to the bird's back, setting her feet on its outstretched wings and tying her sash to one of the strongest feathers. Then the swallow flew high up into the air, over lake and forest, high up over the great mountains of eternal snow. Thumbelina shivered in the cold air, but then she snuggled in under the bird's warm feathers, merely poking out her little head to look at all the loveliness stretched out beneath her.

And at last they reached the warm countries. The sun was shining there much more brightly than with us, and the sky looked twice as far off. On walls and slopes grew the finest black and white grapes, in the woods hung lemons and oranges; the air smelt sweetly of myrtle and curled mint, and the most delightful children darted about on the roads playing with large gay-coloured butterflies. But the swallow kept flying on and on, and the country became more and more beautiful, till at last they came upon an ancient palace of glittering white marble standing among vivid green trees beside a blue lake. Vines went curling up round the tall pillars, and right at the top were a number of swallow's nests. One of these was the home of the swallow that had brought Thumbelina on its back.

"Here's my house," cried the swallow.

"But you see those beautiful flowers growing down here? You shall now choose one of them yourself, and then I'll put you on it, and you can make yourself as cosy as you like."

"That will be lovely," she said, clapping her little hands.

A large white marble column was lying there on the ground just as it had fallen and broken into three pieces, but in among these were growing the most beautiful white flowers. The swallow flew down with Thumbelina and placed her on one of the broad petals – but what a surprise she got! There in the middle of the flower sat a little man as white and transparent as if he had been made of glass. He wore the neatest little gold crown on his head and the most exquisite wings on his shoulders; he himself was no bigger than Thumbelina. He was the guardian spirit of the flower. Each flower had just such a little man or woman living in it, but this one was King of them all.

"Goodness, how handsome he is!" whispered Thumbelina to the swallow. The little monarch was very frightened of the swallow, which of course seemed a gigantic bird beside one so small and delicate as himself; but when he caught sight of Thumbelina he was enchanted, for she was much the prettiest little lady he had ever seen. So he took the gold crown off his head

and placed it on hers. At the same time he asked her what her name was and whether she would be his wife; if so, she would become Queen of all the flowers. Well, he would be a proper husband for her, quite different from the son of the old toad and from the mole with the black velvet coat. So she said yes to the handsome King, and from every flower there appeared a lady or a gentleman that was the most dapper little creature imaginable. Each one brought a present for Thumbelina, but the best of them all was a pair of beautiful wings from a large white fly. These were fastened to her back, so that she too could flit from flower to flower. There was such rejoicing, and the swallow sat up above in its nest and sang for them as well as it could, but the poor bird was really too sad at heart, for it was very fond of Thumbelina and would have liked never to be parted from her.

"You shan't be called Thumbelina," said the guardian spirit of the flower to her. "It's an ugly name, and you are so pretty. We will call you Maia."

"Goodbye, goodbye," said the swallow and flew away again from the warm countries, far away back to Denmark. There it had a little nest above the window where the man lives who can tell fairy tales, and there it was that the swallow sang "Tweet-tweet!" to him ... And that's where the whole story comes from.

THE STAUNCH TIN SOLDIER

*T*here were once twenty-five tin soldiers, all brothers, for they all came from one old tin spoon. "Shoulder arms! Eyes front!" – that's how they were, and they wore splendid red tunics with blue trousers. The very first thing they ever heard, when the lid was taken off the box in which they were lying, was – "tin soldiers!" It was a little boy who shouted this and clapped his hands. He had been given them for his birthday, and now he was putting them up on the table.

Each soldier was the very image of the other, except for one who was a little bit different. He had only one leg, because he was the last to be made and there wasn't enough tin to go round. Still, there he stood, as firmly on his one leg as the others on their two; and, as it happened, he's the soldier this story is all about.

There were a lot of other toys on the table where the tin soldiers had been put up, but the one you noticed first was a beautiful paper castle; through its tiny windows you could see right into the rooms. In front of it were some small trees standing round a little mirror, which was supposed to represent a lake, with wax swans reflected in it as they swam. Everything was very pretty, and yet the prettiest of all was a little lady who was standing at the open door of the castle. She, too, was cut out of paper, but she was wearing a skirt of the clearest muslin and a narrow blue ribbon draped over her shoulder like a scarf, with a glittering spangle in the middle as big as the whole of her face. The little lady was holding out both her arms; you see, she was a dancer and, besides, she had kicked one of her legs so high in the air that the tin soldier couldn't make out where it was and imagined she only had one leg, like himself.

"That's the wife for me!" he thought to himself. "But she's so grand; she lives in a castle. I've only got a box, and there are twenty-five of us to that; it's no place for her. All the same, I must see if I can't get to know her." Then he lay down at full length behind a snuff-box that was on the table. From here he could keep his eyes on the elegant little lady, who continued to stand on one leg without losing her balance.

Later in the evening, all the other tin soldiers went back into their box, and the people in the house went to bed. The toys now began to play games – visiting, fighting, dancing. The tin soldiers rattled in their box, because they wanted to join in, but they couldn't get the lid off. The nutcrackers turned somersaults, and the slate pencil had some fun on the slate. There was such a noise that the canary woke up and began to join in with some twittering in verse. The only two who didn't budge were the tin soldier and the little dancer. She stood perfectly upright on tiptoe with both arms stretched out, while he was just as staunch on his one leg; his eyes never left her for a moment.

Suddenly the clock struck twelve and – clack! flew the lid from the snuff-box, but do you suppose there was snuff in it? No, there was a little black goblin – it was a kind of Jack-in-the-box.

"Tin soldier!" cried the goblin. "Will you please keep your eyes to yourself!" But the tin soldier pretended not to hear.

"All right – you wait till tomorrow!" said the goblin.

And when tomorrow came and the children got up, the tin soldier was put away by the window; and, whether it was the goblin or the draught that did it, all at once the window flew open and the soldier fell out head first from the third storey. It was a terrible fall. There was his leg going straight up in the air, and he was left standing on his helmet with his bayoriet stuck in between the paving-stones.

The maidservant and the little boy came down directly to look for him; but although they very nearly trod on him, they never saw him. If only the tin soldier had called out "Here I am!" they would have found him easily enough; but he didn't think it would be right to shout out, as he was in uniform.

Presently it began raining, more and more heavily, until it was a regular downpour. When it was over, two street-boys came by. "Gosh, look at that! " said one of them. "There's a tin soldier. Let's send him for a sail." So they made a boat out of a newspaper, put the tin soldier aboard, and away he sailed down the gutter with the two boys running alongside and clapping their hands. Bless my soul, how the waves did rock in the gutter, and what a strong current there was! Well, after all, it had been a real soaker. The paper boat bobbed up and down, and now and then it whirled round so fast that the tin soldier became quite dizzy. But he kept staunch and never moved a muscle; he looked straight ahead, and still shouldered arms.

All at once the boat drifted in under a broad culvert; it was as dark as if he were in his box.

"I wonder where I'm coming to now", he thought. "I'll swear it's all the fault of that goblin. If only the little lady were here in the boat, it could be twice as dark for all I'd care!"

Just then a great water-rat appeared, who lived under the culvert. "Where's your passport?" asked the rat. "Now then, show me your passport!"

But the tin soldier never said a word and clutched his gun more tightly than ever. The boat

rushed on, and the rat after it. Ugh! How it ground its teeth and shouted out to sticks and straws: "Stop him! Stop him! He hasn't paid the toll! He hasn't shewn his passport!"

But the current grew stronger and stronger; the tin soldier could already see daylight ahead where the culvert ended. But he could also hear a roaring sound that might well bring dismay to the bravest man. Just think of it – where the culvert ended, the gutter plunged straight out into a large canal. It was as dangerous for him as it would be for us to sail down a big waterfall.

By now he had come so near that there was no stopping. The boat dashed out, the poor tin soldier held himself as stiffly as he could; no one should say that he had moved an eyelid. The boat spun round three or four times and filled right up with water, until it was bound to sink. The tin soldier was now up to his neck; the boat sank deeper and deeper; the paper grew more and more sodden. At last the water closed over the soldier's head ... He thought of the pretty little dancer whom he would never see again, and the old song rang in his ears:

"On, on, brave warrior!
On, where death awaits thee!"

At this moment, the paper went to pieces, and the tin soldier fell right through – but was instantly swallowed by a large fish. Oh, and how dark it was inside! Even worse than it was in the culvert, and so terribly cramped, too. But the tin soldier was still staunch, still shouldering arms, as he lay at full length.

The fish darted about, making the most terrifying twists and turns. Then at last it lay quite still; a lightning flash went through it, there was broad daylight, and someone called out: "A tin soldier!" The fish had been caught, taken to market and sold, and here it was in the kitchen, where the maid cut it open with a big knife. She picked up the soldier by the waist with her two fingers and carried him into the parlour, where everyone wanted to see this extraordinary man who had been travelling about inside a fish. But the tin soldier thought nothing of it. They set him up on the table, and there – well, what wonderful things can happen! The tin soldier found himself in the very same room as he had been in before. There they were – the same children, the same toys on the table, the same beautiful castle with the pretty little dancer who still stood on one leg and kept the other one high in the air – she, too, had been staunch. This touched the tin soldier, who could have wept tears of tin, only that would hardly have done! He looked at her, and she looked at him, but neither of them spoke.

Suddenly one of the small boys took and threw the soldier straight into the stove. He had no reason for doing this; of course, the Jack-in-the-box was behind it all.

The tin soldier stood in a complete glow; the heat that he felt was tremendous, but whether it came from the actual fire or from love, he had no idea. All his bright colours were gone, but no one could tell if this had happened on his voyage or was the result of grief. He looked at the little lady, she looked at him, and he could feel that he was melting, but he still stood staunchly with arms at the shoulder. Then a door opened, the draught caught the dancer, and she flew like a sylph right into the stove to the tin soldier, flared up in a flame and was gone. The tin soldier was melted down to a lump and, when the maid cleared out the ashes next morning, she found him in the shape of a little tin heart; but all that was left of the dancer was her spangle, and that was burnt as black as coal.

THE UGLY DUCKLING

Summertime! How lovely it was out in the country, with the wheat standing yellow, the oats green, and the hay all stacked down in the grassy meadows! And there went the stork on his long red legs, chattering away in Egyptian, for he had learnt that language from his mother. The fields and meadows had large woods all around, and in the middle of the woods there were deep lakes.

Yes, it certainly was lovely out in the country. Bathed in sunshine stood an old manor-house with a deep moat round it, and growing out of the wall down by the water were huge dock-leaves; the biggest of them were so tall that little children could stand upright underneath. The place was as tangled and twisty as the densest forest, and here it was that a duck was sitting on her

nest. It was time for her to hatch out her little ducklings, but it was such a long job that she was beginning to lose patience. She hardly ever had a visitor; the other ducks thought more of swimming about in the moat than of coming and sitting under a dockleaf just for the sake of a quack with her.

At last the eggs cracked open one after the other – "peep! peep!" – and all the yolks had come to life and were sticking out their heads.

"Quack, quack!" said the mother duck, and then the little ones scuttled out as quickly as they could, prying all round under the green leaves; and she let them do this as much as they liked, because green is so good for the eyes.

"Oh, how big the world is!" said the ducklings. And they certainly had much more room now than when they were lying in the egg.

"Do you suppose this is the whole world!" said their mother. "Why, it goes a long way past the other side of the garden, right into the parson's field; but I've never been as far as that. Well, you're all out now, I hope" – and she got up from her nest – "no, not all; the largest egg is still here. How ever long will it be? I can't bother about it much more." And she went on sitting again.

"Well, how's it going?," asked an old duck who came to pay a call.

"There's just this one egg that's taking such a time," said the sitting duck. "It simply won't break. But just look at the others – the loveliest ducklings I've ever seen. They all take after their father – the wretch! Why doesn't he come and see me?"

"Let's have a look at the egg which won't crack," said the old duck. "I'll bet it's a turkey's egg. That's how I was bamboozled once. The little ones gave me no end of trouble, for they were afraid of the water – fancy that! – I just couldn't get them to go in. I quacked and clacked, but it was no good. Lets' have a look at the egg ... Ay, that's turkey's egg, depend upon it! Let it be and teach the others to swim."

"I think I'll sit just a little while yet," said the duck. "I've been sitting so long that it won't hurt to sit a little longer."

"Please yourself!" said the old duck, and away she waddled.

At last the big egg cracked. There was a "peep! peep!" from the young one as he tumbled out, looking so large and ugly. The duck glanced at him and said: "My! what a huge great duckling that is! None of the others look a bit like that. Still, it's never a turkey-chick, I'll be bound

... Well, we shall soon find out. He shall go into the water, if I have to kick him in myself!"

The next day the weather was gloriously fine, with sun shining on all the green dock-leaves. The mother duck with her whole family came down to the moat. Splash! into the water she jumped. "Quack, quack!" she said, and one after another the ducklings plomped in after her. The water closed over their heads, but they were up again in a moment and floated along so

beautifully. Their legs worked of their own accord, and now the whole lot were in the water – even the ugly grey duckling joined in the swimming.

"It's no turkey, that's certain", said the duck. "Look how beautifully he uses his legs and how straight he holds himself. He's my own little one all right, and he's quite handsome, when you really come to look at him. Quack, quack! Now, come along with me and let me show you the

world and introduce you all to the barnyard, but mind and keep, close to me, so that nobody steps on you; and keep a sharp look-out for the cat."

Then they made their way into the duckyard. There was a fearful noise going on, for there were two families fighting for an eel's head, and after all it was the cat that got it.

"You see! That's the way of the world," said the mother duck and licked her bill, for she too had fancied the eel's head. "Now then, where are your legs?" she said, "Look slippy and make a

nice bow to the old duck over there. She's the most genteel of all these; she has Spanish blood, that's why she's so plump. And do you see that crimson rag she wears on one leg? It's extremely fine; it's the highest distinction any duck can win. It's as good as saying that there is no thought of getting rid of her; man and beast are to take notice! Look alive, and don't turn your toes in! A well-bred duckling turns its toes out, like father and mother ... That's it. Now make a bow and say 'quack'!"

They all obeyed; but the other ducks round about looked at them and said out loud: "There! Now we've got to have that rabble as well – as if there weren't enough of us already! Ugh! What a sight that duckling is! We can't possibly put up with him" – and one duck immediately flew at him and bit him in the neck.

"Leave him alone," said the mother. "He's doing no one any harm."

"Yes, but he's so gawky and peculiar," said the one that had pecked him, "so he'll have to be squashed."

"What pretty children you have, my dear!" said the old duck with the rag on her leg. "All of them but one, who doesn't seem right. I only wish you could make him all over again."

"No question of that, my lady," said the ducklings' mother. "He's not pretty, but he's so good-tempered and he can swim just as well as the others – I daresay even a bit better. I fancy his looks will improve as he grows up, or maybe in time he'll grow down a little. He lay too long in the egg – that's why he isn't quite the right shape." And then she plucked his neck for him and smoothed out his feathers. "Anyhow, he's a drake, and so it doesn't matter so much," she added. "I feel sure he'll turn out pretty strong and be able to manage all right".

"The other ducklings are charming," said the old duck. "Make yourselves at home, my dears, and if you should find such a thing as an eel's head you may bring it to me."

And so they made themselves at home.

But the poor duckling who was the last out of the egg and looked so ugly got pecked and jostled and teased by ducks and hens alike. "The great gawk!" they all clucked. And the turkey,

who was born with spurs and therefore thought himself an emperor, puffed up his feathers like a ship under full sail and went straight at him, and then he gobble-gobbled till he was quite red in the face. The poor duckling didn't know where to turn; he was terribly upset over being so ugly and the laughing-stock of the whole barnyard.

That's how it was the first day, and afterwards things grew worse and worse. The poor duckling got chivied about by all of them; even his own brothers and sisters treated him badly, and they kept saying: "If only the cat would get you, you ridiculous great guy!" And the mother herself wished he were far away. The ducks nipped him, the hens pecked him, and the maid who had to feed the poultry let fly at him with her foot.

After that, he ran away and fluttered over the hedge, and the little birds in the bushes grew frightened and flew into the air. "That's because I'm so ugly," thought the duckling and closed his eyes – and yet managed to get away. Eventually he came out to the great marsh where the wildducks lived and lay there all night, utterly tired and dispirited.

In the morning the wild-ducks flew up and looked at their new companion. "What ever are you?" they asked, and the duckling turned in every direction and bowed as well as he could.

"What a scarecrow you are!" said the wild-ducks, "but that won't matter to us, as long as you don't marry into our family." Poor thing! He wasn't dreaming of getting married; all he wanted was to be allowed to stay quietly among the rushes and drink a little marsh-water. Alter he had been there for two whole days, two wild-geese came along – or rather two wild-ganders, for they were both males. It was not long since they were hatched; that's why they were so perky.

"Look here, my lad!" they began. "You are so ugly that we quite like you. Will you come in with us and migrate? Not far off, in another marsh, are some very nice young wild-geese, none of them married, who can quack beautifully. Here's a chance for you to make a hit, ugly as you are."

"Bang! bang!" suddenly echoed above them, and both the ganders fell down dead in the rushes, and the water became red with blood. "Bang! bang!" sounded once more, and flocks of wild-geese flew up from the rushes, so that immediately fresh shots rang out. A big shoot was on. The party lay ready all round the marsh; some even sat up in the trees on the branches that stretched right out over the rushes. Clouds of blue smoke drifted in among the dark trees and hung far over the water. Splashing through the mud came the gun-dogs, bending back reeds and rushes this way and that. It was terrifying for the poor duckling, who was just turning his head round to bury it under his wing when he suddenly found close beside him a fearsome great dog with lolling tongue and grim, glittering eyes. It lowered its muzzle right down to the duckling, bared its sharp teeth and – splash! it went off again without touching him.

The duckling gave a sigh of relief. "Thank goodness, I'm so ugly that even the dog doesn't

fancy the taste of me." And he lay there quite still, while the shot pattered on the reeds and crack after crack was heard from the guns.

It was late in the day before everything was quiet again, but the poor duckling didn't dare to get up yet; he waited several hours longer before he took a look round and then made off from

the marsh as fast as he could go. Over field and meadow he scuttled, but there was such a wind that he found it difficult to get along.

Towards evening he came up to a poor little farm-cottage; it was so broken-down that it hardly knew which way to fall, and so it remained standing. The wind whizzed so fiercely round the duckling that he had to sit on his tail so as not to be blown over. The wind grew worse and worse. Then he noticed that the door had come off one of its hinges and hung so much on the slant that he could slip into the house through the crack. And that's just what he did.

There was an old woman living here with her cat and her hen. The cat, whom she called Sonny, could arch its back and purr; it could even give out sparks, if you stroked its fur the wrong way. The hen had such short little legs that it was called Chickabiddy Shortlegs; it was a very good layer, and the woman loved it like her own child.

Next morning they at once noticed the strange duckling, and the cat started to purr and the hen to cluck. "Why, what's up?" said the woman, looking round. But her sight wasn't very good, and she took the duckling for at fat duck that had lost its way. "My! What a find!" she said. "I shall be able to have duck's eggs – as long as it isn't a drake! We must give it a trial."

And so the duckling was taken on trial for three weeks; but there was no sign of an egg. Now, the cat was master in the house and the hen was mistress, and they always used to say "We and the world," because they fancied that they made up half the world – what's more, much the superior half of it. The duckling thought there might be two opinions about that, but the hen wouldn't hear of it.

"Can you lay eggs?" she asked.

"No."

"Well, then, hold your tongue, will you!"

And the cat asked: "Can you arch your back or purr or give out sparks?"

"No."

"Well, then, your opinion's not wanted, when sensible people are talking."

And the duckling sat in the corner, quite out of spirits. Then suddenly he remembered the fresh air and the sunshine, and he got such a curious longing to swim in the water that – he couldn't help it – he had to tell the hen.

"What's the matter with you?" she asked. "You haven't anything to do – that's why you get these fancies. They'd soon go, if only you'd lay eggs or else purr."

"But it's so lovely to swim in the water", said the duckling; "so lovely to duck your head in it and dive down to the bottom."

"Most enjoyable, I'm sure," said the hen.

"You must have gone crazy. Ask the cat about it – I've never met any one as clever as he is – ask him if he's fond of swimming or diving! I say nothing of myself. Ask our old mistress, the wisest woman in the world! Do you suppose that she's keen on swimming and diving?"

"You don't understand me," said the duckling.

"Well, if we don't understand you, I should like to know who would. Surely you'll never try and make out you are wiser than the cat and the mistress – not to mention myself. Don't be silly, child! Give thanks to your Maker for all the kindness you have met with. Haven't you come to a nice warm room, where you have company that can teach you something? But you're just a stupid, and there's no fun in having you here. You may take my word for it – if I say unpleasant things to you, it's all for your good; that's just how you can tell which are your real friends. Only see that you lay eggs and learn how to purr or give out sparks!"

"I think I'll go out into the wide world," said the duckling.

"Yes, do," said the hen.

And so the duckling went off. He swam in the water; he dived down; but none of them would have anything to do with him because of his ugliness.

Autumn now set in. The leaves in the wood turned yellow and brown, the wind seized them and whirled them about, while the sky above had a frosty look. The clouds hung heavy with hail and snow, and the raven who perched on the fence kept squawking "ow! ow!" – he felt so cold. The very thought of it gave you the shivers. Yes, the poor duckling was certainly having a bad time.

One evening, when there was a lovely sunset, a whole flock of large handsome birds appeared out of the bushes. The duckling had never seen such beautiful birds, all glittering white with long graceful necks.

They were swans. They gave the most extraordinary cry, spread out their magnificent long wings and flew from this cold country away to warmer lands and open lakes.

They mounted high, high up into the air, and the ugly little duckling felt so strange as he watched them. He turned round and round in the water like a wheel and craned his neck in their direction, letting out a cry so shrill and strange that it quite scared even himself. Ah! he could never forget those beautiful, fortunate birds; and directly they were lost to sight he dived right down to the bottom and, when he came up again, he was almost beside himself. He had no idea what the birds were called, nor where they were flying to, and yet they were dearer to him, than any he had ever known; he didn't envy them in the least – how could he ever dream of such loveliness for himself? He would be quite satisfied, if only the ducks would just put up with him, poor gawky-looking creature!

What a cold winter it was! The duckling had to keep swimming about in the water to prevent it freezing right up. But every night, the pool he was swimming in grew smaller and smaller; then the ice froze so hard that you could hear it creaking. The duckling had to keep his feet moving all the time to prevent the water from closing up. At last he grew faint with exhaustion and lay quite still and finally froze fast in the ice.

Early next morning he was seen by a peasant who went out and broke the ice with his wooden clog and carried the duckling home to his wife. And there they revived him.

The children wanted to play with him, but the duckling was afraid they meant mischief and fluttered in panic right up into the milkbowl, so that the milk slopped over into the room. The woman screamed out and clapped her hands in the air, and then he flew into the butter-tub, and from there down into the flour-bin, and out of it again. Dear, dear, he did look an object! The woman screamed at him and hit at him with the tongs, and the children tumbled over each other trying to catch him – how they laughed and shouted! ... It was a good thing the door was open; the duckling darted out into the bushes and sank down, dazed, in the new-fallen snow.

But it would be far too dismal to describe all the want and misery the duckling had to go through during that hard winter ... He was sheltering among the reeds on the marsh, when the sun began to get warm again and the larks to sing; beautiful spring had arrived.

Then all at once he tried his wings; the whirr of them was louder than before, and they carried him swiftly away. Almost before he realized it, he found himself in a big garden with apple-trees in blossom and sweetsmelling lilac that dangled from long green boughs right over the winding stream. Oh, it was so lovely here in all the freshness of spring! And straight ahead, out of the thicket, came three beautiful white swans, ruffling their feathers and floating so lightly on the water. The duckling recognized the splendid creatures and was overcome with a strange feeling of melancholy.

"I will fly across to them, those royal birds! They will peck me to death for daring, ugly as I am, to go near them. Never mind! Better to be killed by them than be nipped by the ducks, pecked by the hens, kicked by the girl who minds the poultry, and suffer hardship in winter." And he flew out on to the water and swam towards the beautiful swans. As they caught sight of him, they darted with ruffled feathers to meet him. "Yes, kill me, kill me!" cried the poor creature and bowed his head to the water awaiting death. But what did he see there in the clear stream? It was a reflection of himself that he saw in front of him, but no longer a clumsy greyish bird, ugly and unattractive – no, he was himself a swan!

It doesn't matter about being born in a duckyard, as long as you are hatched from a swan's egg.

He felt positively glad at having gone through so much hardship and want; it helped him to appreciate all the happiness and beauty that were there to welcome him ... And the three great swans swam round and round and stroked him with their beaks.

Some little children came into the garden and threw bread and grain into the water, and the smallest one called out: "There's a new swan!" and the other children joined in with shouts of delight: "Yes, there's a new swan!" And they clapped their hands and danced about and ran to fetch father and mother. Bits of bread and cake were thrown into the water, and everyone said "The new one is the prettiest – so young and handsome!" And the old swans bowed before him.

This made him feel quite shy, and he tucked his head away under his wing – he himself hardly knew why. He was too, too happy, but not a bit proud, for a good heart is never proud. He thought of how he had been despised and persecuted, and now he heard everybody saying that he was the loveliest of all lovely birds. And the lilacs bowed their branches to him right down to the water, and the sunshine felt so warm and kindly. Then he ruffled his feathers, raised his slender neck and rejoiced from his heart: "I never dreamed of so much happiness, when I was the ugly duckling."

THE SWINEHERD

Once upon a time there was a prince who hadn't much money, but he had a kingdom; and though this was quite small, it was large enough to marry on, and marry he would.

Still, it was really rather bold of him to say straight out to the Emperor's daughter: "Will you have me?" But sure enough he did, for his name was famous everywhere, and there were hundreds of princesses who would only too gladly have taken him. But do you think she did? Well, now just listen. Growing on the grave of the Prince's father was a rosetree – oh, such a lovely rose-tree. It only flowered every five years, and even then had but one solitary bloom. But this rose smelt so sweet that it made you forget all your cares and troubles. And the Prince also had a nightingale that could sing just as if it had all the loveliest tunes hidden away in its little throat. The Princess should have both the rose and the nightingale, he said; and so they were placed in big silver caskets and sent to her.

The Emperor had them brought before him in the great hall, where the Princess was playing "visitors" with her maids-of-honour. They never did anything else and, when she saw the big caskets with the presents inside, she clapped her hands with glee.

"I do hope it's a pussy-cat," she said ... But then out came the lovely rose.

"Oh, isn't it pretty!" cried all the maids-of-honour.

"It's more than pretty," said the Emperor, "it's handsome."

But when the Princess touched it she nearly burst into tears. "Oh, Papa, what a shame!" she cried. "It's not artificial, it's real!"

"Come, let's first see what's in the other casket before we get annoyed," suggested the Emperor. And then out came the nightingale. Its singing was so lovely that for the moment there wasn't a thing that could be said against it.

"*Superbe! Charmant!*" exclaimed the maids-of-honour, for they all talked French, the one worse than the other. "How the bird reminds me of Her late Majesty's musicalbox!" said an old courtier. "Dear me, yes! Exactly the same tone, the same expression!"

"So it is," said the Emperor; and he cried like a child.

"All the same, I can't believe that it's real," said the Princess.

"Yes, it is; it's a real live bird," said the ones who had brought it.

"All right, then let it fly away," said the Princess, and she wouldn't hear of the Prince being allowed to come.

But he wasn't going to be put off like that. He smeared his face with brown and black, pulled his cap down over his eyes and knocked at the door. "Good morning, Emperor!" he said. "I wonder if you've got a job for me here at the Castle."

"Ah, well," said the Emperor, "there are so many who come and ask that. But now, let me see – yes, I want someone to mind the pigs. We've such a lot of pigs."

And so the Prince was appointed Imperial Swineherd. He was given a miserable little room down by the pig-sties, and there he had to live. But all day he sat working, and by the evening he had made a lovely little pot with bells round it and, as soon as the pot boiled, these tinkled charmingly; they played the old tune of –

"Ah, my dear Augustine.
Our dreams are all done, done, done!"

But the cunningest arrangement of all was that, if you held your finger in the steam from the pot, you could at once smell what was being cooked on every fire in the town. Well, of course, that was something quite different from a rose.

Presently the Princess came strolling along with all her court-ladies, and when she heard the music she stopped, looking so delighted; for she, too, could play "Ah, my dear Augustine" – it was the only tune she knew, and she played it with one finger.

"Why, that's *my* tune!" she said. "This pigman must be a man of taste. Look here, go in and ask him how much he wants for the instrument."

So one of the court-ladies had to run in and see him; but she put on her clogs first.

"How much do you want for that pot?" she asked.

"I want ten kisses from the Princess," answered the pigman.

"Goodness gracious!" said the maid-of-honour.

"That's the price; I can't take less," said the pigman.

"Well, what does he say?" asked the Princess.

"I really can't repeat it," said the maid-of-honour. "It's too dreadful."

"Well, then whisper it" – and the maid-of-honour whispered it.

"Oh, how rude he is!" said the Princess and walked off at once. But when she had gone a little way, the bells began to tinkle so charmingly –

"Ah, my dear Augustine,
    our dreams are all done, done, done!"

"Come," said the Princess, "ask him if he will take ten kisses from my ladies-in-waiting."

"No, thank you," said the pigman. "Ten kisses from the Princess, or I stick to my pot!"

"How horribly annoying!" said the Princess. "Well, then, you ladies'll have to stand in front of me, so that no one can see."

The court-ladies went and stood in front of her, spreading out their dresses; and then the pigman had his ten kisses and she got her pot.

Goodness! What fun they had! Day and night the pot was kept on the boil. There wasn't a kitchen in the town where they didn't know what was being cooked, whether it was the Mayor's or the shoemaker's. The maids-of-honour danced about, clapping their hands with glee.

"We know who's going to have soup and pancakes, and we know who's going to have chops and jelly. It's so interesting."

"Most interesting," observed the high Stewardess.

"Yes, but not a word to anyone, mind you; for I'm the Emperor's daughter."

"O, dear, no!" they all replied. "We shouldn't dream of it."

The swineherd – that is to say, the Prince, but you see, they didn't know but what he was a regular pigman – couldn't let the day go by without making something. The next thing he made was a rattle. When you swung it round, it played all the waltzes and jigs and polkas that anybody had ever heard of.

"Now that really is *superbe,*" said the Princess, as she was passing. "I've never heard anything lovelier. Look here, go in and ask him what he wants for that instrument. But, mind, no kisses!"

"He wants a hundred kisses from the Princess," said the lady-in-waiting who had been in to ask.

"The fellow must be mad," said the Princess and began to walk off. But when she had gone a little way, she stopped. "Art must be encouraged," she said; "after all, I'm the Emperor's daughter. Tell him he shall have ten kisses like yesterday, and my ladies-in-waiting will give him the rest."

"Oh, but we couldn't bear to do that," said the ladies.

"Nonsense!" said the Princess. "If I can kiss him, so can you. Remember, I give you wages and board" – and once more the maid-of-honour had to go in and see the pigman.

"A hundred kisses from the Princess," he said, "or we stay as we are."

"Stand in front!" she cried. And so all the court-ladies placed themselves in front, and the kissing began.

"What on earth are they all up to over there by the sties!" said the Emperor, who had just stepped out on to his balcony. He rubbed his eyes and put on his spectacles. "Why, it's the ladies-in-waiting, up to some game or other. Perhaps I'd better go and have a look" – and he gave a hitch to the back of his slippers, for he had trodden them down at the heel.

Phew! What a hurry he was in!

As soon as he came down into the courtyard, he crept along very quietly. And the maids-of-honour were so busy counting the kisses, for it had to be fair do's – he mustn't have too many kisses, nor yet too few – that they never noticed the Emperor, who now drew himself up on tiptoe.

"What's all this!" he said, when he saw them kissing; and he slogged them over the head with his slipper, just as the young pigman was having his eighty-sixth kiss. "Out you get!" said the Emperor, for he was furious, and both Princess and swineheard were turned out of his kingdom.

Look, there she sat crying, while the swineherd scolded and the rain came down in torrents.

"Poor me!" said the Princess. "If only I had accepted the handsome Prince! Oh, I am so unhappy!"

The swineherd went behind a tree, wiped off the black and brown from his face, threw away his old clothes and now stepped forward in princely robes that were so magnificent that the Princess couldn't help making a curtsey.

"My dear, I've come to despise you," he said. "An honest prince you rejected. The rose and the nightingale were not to your taste. But the swineherd – you could kiss him for the sake of a musical box. Now you can have what you asked for!"

And with that he went into his kingdom, shut the door and bolted it; but she could stand outside if she cared to and sing –

"Ah, my dear Augustine,
Our dreams are all done, done, done!"

THE LITTLE MATCH-SELLER

It was terribly cold. Snow was falling and soon it would be quite dark; for it was the last day in the year – New Year's Eve. Along the street, in that same cold and dark, went a poor little girl in bare feet – well, yes, it's true, she had slippers on when she left home; but what was the good of that?

They were great big slippers which her mother used to wear, so you can imagine the size of them; and they both came off when the little girl scurried across the road just as two carts went whizzing by at a fearful rate. One slipper was not to be found, and a boy ran off with the other, saying it would do for a cradle one day when he had children of his own.

So there was the little girl walking along in her bare feet that were simply blue with cold. In an old apron she was carrying a whole lot of matches, and she had one bunch of them in her hand. She hadn't sold anything all day, and no one had given her a single penny. Poor mite, she looked so downcast as she trudged along hungry and shivering. The snowflakes settled on her long flaxen hair, which hung in pretty curls over her shoulder; but you may be sure she wasn't thinking about her looks. Lights were shining in every window, and out into the street came the lovely smell of roast goose. You see, it was New Year's Eve; that's what she was thinking about.

Over in a little corner between two houses – one of them
jutted out rather more into the street than the other – there
she crouched and huddled with her legs tucked under her;

93

but she only got colder and colder. She didn't dare to go home, for she hadn't sold a match nor earned a single penny. Her father would beat her, and besides it was so cold at home. They had only the bare roof over their heads and the wind whistled through that although the worst cracks had been stopped up with rags and straw.

Her hands were really quite numb with cold. Ah, but a little match – that would be a comfort. If only she dared pull one out of the bunch, just one, strike it on the wall and warm her fingers! She pulled one out ... ritch! ... how it spirted and blazed! Such a clear warm flame, like a little candle, as she put her hand round it – yes, and what a curious light it was! The little girl fancied she was sitting in front of a big iron stove with shiny brass knobs and brass facings, with such a warm friendly fire burning ... why, whatever was that?

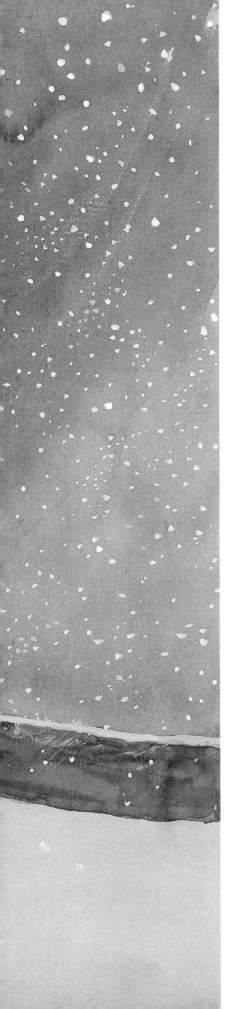

She was just stretching out her toes, so as to warm them too, when – out went the flame, and the stove vanished. There she sat with a little stub of burnt-out match in her hand.

She struck another one. It burned up so brightly, and where the gleam fell on the wall this became transparent like gauze. She could see right into the room, where the table was laid with a glittering white cloth and with delicate china; and there, steaming deliciously, was the roast goose stuffed with prunes and apples. Then, what was even finer, the goose jumped off the dish and waddled along the floor with the carvingknife and fork in its back. Right up to the poor little girl it came ... but then the match went out, and nothing could be seen but the massive cold wall.

She lighted another match. Now she was sitting
under the loveliest Christmas tree; it was even bigger
and prettier than the one she had seen through the glass-
door at the rich merchant's at Christmas. Hundreds of
candles were burning on the green branches, and gay-
coloured prints, like the ones they hang in the shop-
windows, looked down at her. The little girl reached
up both her hands ... then the match went out; all the
Christmas candles rose higher and higher, until now
she could see they were the shining stars. One of them
rushed down the sky with a long fiery streak.

"That's somebody dying," said the little girl, for her dead Grannie, who was the only one who had been kind to her, had told her that a falling star shows that a soul is going up to God.

She struck yet another match on the wall. It gave a glow all around, and there in the midst of it stood her old grandmother, looking so very bright and gentle and loving. "Oh, Grannie," cried the little girl, "do take me with you! I know you'll disappear as soon as the match goes out – just as the warm stove did, and the lovely roast goose, and the wonderful great Christmas-tree".

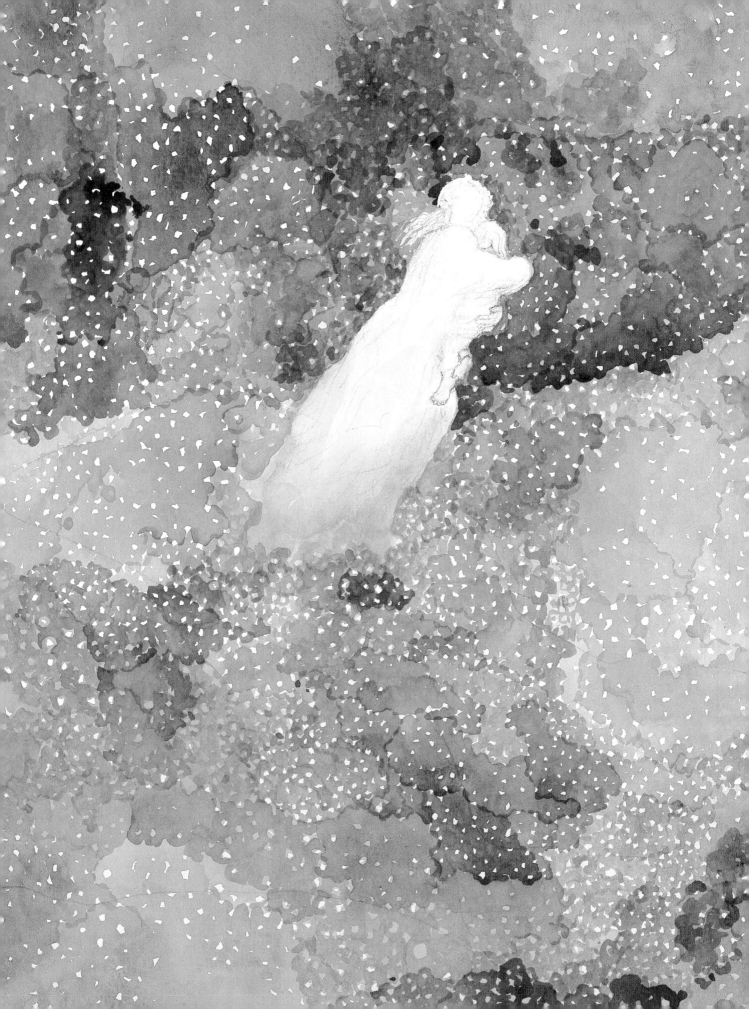

And she quickly struck the rest of the matches in the bunch, for she did so want to keep her Grannie there. And the matches flared up so gloriously that it became brighter than broad daylight. Never had Grannie looked so tall and beautiful. She took the little girl into her arms, and together they flew in joy and splendour, up, up, to where there was no cold, no hunger, no fear. They were with God.

But in the cold early morning huddled between the two houses, sat the little girl with rosy cheeks and a smile on her lips, frozen to death on the last night of the old year. The New Year dawned on the little dead body leaning there with the matches, one lot of them nearly all used up. "She was trying to get warm," people said. Nobody knew what lovely things she had seen and in what glory she had gone with her old Grannie to the happiness of the New Year.

THE EMPEROR'S NEW CLOTHES

$\mathcal{M}$any years ago there lived an Emperor who was so tremendously fond of fine new clothes that he spent all his money on being elegantly dressed. He took no interest in his army or the theatre or in driving through the country, unless it was to shew off his new clothes. He had different clothes for every hour of the day and, just as you might say of a King that he was in the council-chamber, so it was always said of the Emperor: "He's in his wardrobe."

There was plenty of fun going on in the city where the Emperor lived. Strangers were continually arriving, and one day there came two swindlers. They made out they were weavers and could weave the very finest stuffs imaginable. Not only were colours and design unusually attractive, but the clothes made from their material had the peculiarity of being invisible to anyone who wasn't fit for his post or who was hopelessly stupid.

"I say! They must be wonderful clothes," thought the Emperor. "If I had some, I could find out which of my statesmen were unfit for their posts and also be able to tell the clever ones from the stupid. Yes, I must have some of that stuff woven for me at once." And he paid down a large sum of money to the swindlers straight away, so as to enable them to start work.

And they did; they put up a couple of looms and pretended to be working, although there was absolutely nothing in the loom. They cooly demanded the most delicate silk and the finest gold thread, which they promptly stowed away in their own bags; and then they went on working far into the night at their empty looms.

"Well, now, I wonder how they are getting on with the work," said the Emperor to himself. But there was one point that really made him feel rather anxious, namely, that a man who was stupid or quite unfit for his post would never be able to see what was woven. Not that he need have any fears for himself – he was quite confident about that – but all the same it might be better to send someone else first, to find out how things were going. Everyone in the city had heard of the mysterious power possessed by the material, and they were all eager to discover how incapable or stupid his neighbour was.

"I'll send my honest old Prime Minister to the weavers," thought the Emperor. "He's the best one to see what the stuff looks like, for he has plenty of sense and nobody fills his post better than he does."

So off went the honest old Premier to the workshop where the two swindlers sat busy at their empty looms. "Lor' bless my soul," thought the Minister with eyes starting out of his head. "Why, I can't see anything!" But he was careful not to say so.

The two swindlers begged him to take a closer look – didn't he find the colours and design most attractive? They then pointed to the empty loom but, although the poor old Minister opened his eyes wider and wider, he couldn't see a thing; for there wasn't a thing to see. "Good Lord!" he thought, "is it possible that I'm stupid? I never suspected that, and not a soul must hear of it. Can it be that I'm unfit for my post? No, it will never do for me to say that I can't see the material."

"Well, what do you think of it?" asked the one who pretended to be weaving.

"Oh, it's charming! Quite exquisite!" said the old Minister, looking through his spetacles. "What a pattern and what colouring! I shall certainly tell the Emperor how pleased I am with it."

"Ah, we're glad to hear that," said the swindlers, and they then gave details of the colours and the peculiar design. The old Minister listened carefully, so as to be able to repeat all this when he came back to the Emperor – which he duly did.

The swindlers now demanded more money, more silk and more gold thread, for these would be required for weaving. They put it all into their own pockets – not a thread came into the loom – while they went on working the empty frames as before.

By and by, the Emperor sent another honest official to see how the weaving was getting on and whether the stuff wouldn't soon be ready. The same thing happened to him as to the Minister: he looked and looked but, as nothing was there but the empty looms, he couldn't see anything.

"There, isn't it a handsome piece!" said the swindlers, as they pointed out the beauty of the design which wasn't there at all.

"I know I'm not stupid," thought the man, "so it must be my fine position I'm not fit for. Some people might think that rather funny, but I must take good care they don't get to hear of it." And then he praised the material which he couldn't see and assured them of his delight in its charming shades and its beautiful design. "Yes, it's quite exquisite," he said to the Emperor, when he got back.

The splendid material became the talk of the Town. And now the Emperor himself said he must see it while it was still in the loom. Quite a throng of select people, including the two honest old officials who had been there already, went with him to where both the crafty swindlers were now weaving for all they were worth without the vestige of a thread.

"Look, isn't it magnificent!" said the two honest officials. "If Your Majesty will but glance – what a pattern, what colouring!" And they pointed to the empty loom, feeling certain that the others could see the material.

"What's this?" thought the Emperor. "I can't see anything – this is appalling! Am I stupid? Am I not fit to be Emperor? This is the most terrible thing that could happen to me ... Oh, it's quite wonderful," he said to them; "it has our most gracious approval." And he gave a satisfied nod, as he looked at the empty loom; he wasn't going to say that he couldn't see anything. All the courtiers who had come with him looked and looked, but they made no more of it than the rest had done. Still, they all said just what the Emperor said – "Oh, it's quite wonderful!" – and they advised him to have some clothes made from this splendid new material and to wear them for the first time in the grand procession that was shortly taking place. "Magnificent!" "Delightful!" "Superb!" were the comments that ran from mouth to mouth; everyone was so intensely pleased with it. On each of the swindlers the Emperor bestowed a knighthood, with a badge to wear in his button-hole, and the title of Imperial Weaver.

On the eve of the procession the swindlers sat up all night with something like twenty lighted candles. People could see how busy they were finishing off the Emperor's new clothes. They pretended to take the stuff off the loom, they clipped away at the air with huge scissors, they worked at their needles without thread, and last they announced: "There! The Emperor's clothes are ready!"

Then the Emperor, with his most distinguished gentlemen-in-waiting, went in person to the weavers, who each put out his arm just as if he were holding something and said: "Here are the Breeches! Here is the Robe! Here is the Mantle!" And so on. "They are all as light as gossamer; you can hardly feel you have anything on – that's just the beauty of them."

"Yes, indeed," answered the gentlemen-in-waiting. But they couldn't see a thing, for there wasn't a thing to see.

"Now will Your Imperial Majesty be graciously pleased to take off your clothes?" said the swindlers. "Then we can fit you with the new ones, there in front of the big glass."

So the Emperor took off the clothes he was wearing, and the swindlers pretended to hand him each of the new garments they were supposed to have made, and they took him at the waist as if they were fastening something on ... it was the train, and the Emperor turned and twisted in front of the looking-glass.

"Goodness! How well they suit your Majesty! What a wonderful fit!" they all exclaimed. "What a cut! What colours! What sumptuous robes!"

The Master of Ceremonies came in with an announcement. "The canopy to be carried above Your Majesty in the procession is waiting outside."

"All right, I'm ready," said the Emperor. "Aren't they a nice fit!" And he turned round once more in front of the glass, for he really had to make them think he was gazing at his fine clothes.

The chamberlains who were to carry the train groped about on the floor as if they were picking the train up; and, as they walked, they held out their hands, not daring to let it be thought that they couldn't see anything.

There marched the Emperor in the procession under the beautiful canopy, and everybody in the streets and at the windows said: "Goodness! The Emperor's new clothes are the finest he has ever had. What a wonderful train! What a perfect fit!" No one would let it be thought that he couldn't see anything, because that would have meant he wasn't fit for his job, or that he was very stupid. Never had the Emperor's clothes been such a success.

"But he hasn't got anything on!" said a little child. "Goodness gracious, do you hear what the little innocent says?" cried the father; and the child's remark was whispered from one to the other.

"He hasn't got anything on! There's a little child saying he hasn't got anything on!"

"Well, but he hasn't got anything on!" the people all shouted at last. And the Emperor felt most uncomfortable, for it seemed to him that the people were right. But somehow he thought to himself: "I must go through with it now, procession and all." And he drew himself up still more proudly, while his chamberlains walked after him carrying the train that wasn't there.

THE TINDER-BOX

$\mathcal{L}$eft, right! Left right! ... Down the countryroad came a soldier marching. Left, right! Left, right! ... He had his knapsack on his back and a sword at his side, for he had been at the war, and now he was on his way home. But then he met an old witch on the road. Oh! she was ugly – her lower lip hung right down on her chest. "Good evening, soldier," she said, "what a nice sword you've got, and what a big knapsack! You're a proper soldier! Now I'll show you how to get as much money as you want!" "Thank you very much, old dame!" said the soldier.

"Do you see that big tree over there?" said the witch, pointing to a tree near by. "It's quite hollow inside. Now, you must climb right up it, and then you'll see a hole; slip through this, and you'll come deep down into the tree. I will tie a rope round your waist, so that I can haul you up again, as soon as you give me a shout."

"But what am I to do down in the tree?" asked the soldier.

"Fetch money!" answered the witch. "For, mind you, when you get down to the bottom of the tree, you will find yourself in a large passage. It's quite light there, because hundreds of lamps are burning there. Next, you will see three doors; you can open them all right, for the key's in the lock. If you go into the first room, you will see in the middle of the floor a big chest, with a dog sitting on it which has got eyes as big as tea-cups; but never you mind about that! I'll give you my blue-check apron, and you can spread it out on the floor. Then go along quickly and lift off the dog and put it on my apron;

open the lid of the chest and take just as many pennies as you like. They are all copper, but if you would rather have silver, then you must go into the next room. There sits a dog with eyes as large as mill-wheels, but never you mind about that! Put the dog down on my apron, and help yourself to the money! And yet, if it's gold you want, you can get that too – as much as ever you can carry – if only you go into the third roo m. But this time the dog which is sitting on the money-chest has two eyes each one as big as the Round Tower … Something like a dog, I can tell you! But never you mind a bit about that! Just put the dog down on my apron, and then it won't do you any harm, and you can take as much gold out of the chest as you like."

"That doesn't sound at all bad," said the soldier. "But tell me, old witch, what am I to give you? Because I expect you'll be wanting your share!"

"No," said the witch, "not a single penny will I take. You've simply got to bring me an old tinder-box that my grandmother forgot when she was last down there."

"Oh, come on, then! let me get that rope round my middle!" said the soldier.

"Here it is", said the witch, "and here's my blue-check apron."

Then the soldier crawled up the tree, let himself down, plump! through the hole, and now he was standing, as the witch had said, down in the great passage where the hundreds of lamps were burning.

Then he utilocked the first door. Ugh! there sat the dog with eyes as big as tea-cups and glared at him.

"You are a nice chap, you are!" said the soldier. He put it down on the witch's apron and took just as many copper pennies as he could stuff into his pocket. Then he shut the chest, put the dog up again and went into the second room. Bless my soul! there sat the dog with eyes as big as millwheels.

"You shouldn't stare at me so!" said the soldier; "you'll strain your eyes." And then he put the dog down on the witch's apron; but when he saw such piles of silver in the chest, he threw away all the coppers he had got and filled up his pocket and his knapsack with nothing but silver. And now he went into the third room! ... Oh, but it was horrible! The dog in there had actually got two great eyes as big as the Round Tower, and they were going round and round in its head like wheels!

126

"Good evening!" said the soldier; and he touched his cap, because never in his life had he seen such a dog. But after he had looked at it for a bit, he thought to himself, "enough of that!" and went and lifted the dog down on to the floor and opened the chest – why, goodness gracious, what a lot of gold there was! There was enough for him to buy the whole of Copenhagen, all the sugar-pigs that the cake-women sell, and the tinsoldiers and whips and rocking-horses in the world. Yes, yes, plenty of money in there – my word, there was!

So at once the soldier emptied out all the silver coins from his pockets and his knapsack and put in gold instead; yes, and he filled up everything with gold, his pockets, his knapsack, his cap and even his boots, so that he could hardly walk. Now he had got some money! He put the dog back on the chest, slammed the door, and then shouted up through the tree, "hi, mother, haul me up again, will you?"

"Have you got the tinder-box?" asked the witch.

"Oh no! that's true, I had clean forgotten it," said the soldier; and he went straight back and fetched it. The witch hauled him up out of the tree, and there he was again, standing on the road with his pockets, boots, cap and knapsack bulging with money.

"What are you going to do with this tinderbox?" asked the soldier.

"That's no business of yours!" answered the

witch. "You've got your money; now just give me my tinder-box!"

"Rubbish!" said the soldier. "Tell me at once what you want to do with it – or I'll have out my sword and cut your head off."

"No," said the witch.

So he cut off her head ... There she lay!

But the soldier tied up all his money in her apron and made a bundle of it, to go on his back. He put the tinder-box in his pocket and went straight on into the town.

It was a fine town, and he put up at the finest inn. He ordered the very best rooms and the food he was most fond of; for, now that he had all that money, he was a rich man. The servant who had to clean his boots thought, well, this was a funny old pair of boots for such a rich gentleman to have; but he hadn't yet bought any new ones. The next day he went out and got some good boots and some really smart clothes. And now the soldier had become quite a fashionable gentleman, and they told him all about the sights of their town, and about their King, and what a pretty Princess his daughter was.

"Where is she to be seen?" asked the soldier.

"She just isn't to be seen," they all answered. "She lives in a big copper castle with lots of walls and towers all round it. No one but the King is allowed to go to her there, because a fortune-teller once said that she is to marry a common soldier, and the King doesn't like that at all."

"My word! I should like to see her," thought the soldier; but of course he couldn't possibly get leave to.

And now he lived a merry life.

He was always going to the theatre, or driving in the Park; and he gave away lots of money to the poor. That was very nice of him; you see, he remembered so well from the old days how awful it was to be absolutely penniless. But now he was rich and well-dressed, and so he made lots of friends who all said what a fine fellow he was – a real gentleman – and the soldier liked that very much. But as he was spending money every day and never getting any back, at last he had only got twopence left; and so he had to move from the fine rooms he had been living in and go and live in a little poky attic right under the roof. He had to clean his own boots and mend them with a darning-needle, and none of his friends ever came to see him, for there were such a lot of stairs to climb.

One evening, when it was quite dark and he couldn't even buy himself a candle, he suddenly remembered that there was a little bit of candle left in the tinder-box that he had got for the old witch out of the tinder-box and the bit of candle; but just as he was striking a light and the sparks flew up from the flint, the door sprang open, and the dog he had seen down in the tree with eyes as big as tea-cups stood before him and said "What are my lord's commands?"

"I say!" said the soldier. "This must be a queer sort of tinder-box, if I can get whatever I want like that." "Bring me some money," he said to the dog; then flick! and away it went, and flick! here it was back again, with a large bagful of pennies in its mouth.

And now the soldier realised what a splendid tinder-box it was. One stroke brought before him the dog which sat on the chest with the copper money; two strokes, the dog with the silver; and three strokes, the dog with the gold. The soldier lost no time in changing back into the fine rooms and the smart clothes, and of course all his friends remembered him again at once and were tremendously fond of him.

And then one day he thought to himself, "There's something queer about this, that no one's allowed to see the Princess. She's supposed to be so very lovely, according to all these people; but

what's the good of that, if she has to sit the whole time inside the copper castle, the one that has all those towers? Can't I possibly manage to see her somehow? Now then, where's my tinder-box?" So he struck a light and flick! there stood the dog with the eyes as big as tea-cups.

"Of course I know it's the middle of the night," said the soldier, "but all the same I would like to see the Princess, that I would! Just for half a jiffy!"

The dog was out of the door in a flash and, before the soldier had time to think about it, there was the dog again with the Princess lying asleep on his back; and she looked so lovely that anyone could see she was a real princess; and the soldier simply couldn't resist, he had to kiss her – he was a soldier all over.

Then the dog scuttled back again with the Princess, but in the morning, when the King and Queen were at breakfast, the Princess said she had had such a curious dream in the night, about a dog and a soldier. She had ridden on the dog's back, and the soldier had kissed her.

"That's a pretty tale, if you like!" said the Queen.

And so one of the old ladies-in-waiting was told to sit up the following night by the Princess' bed and see if it was really a dream or not.

The soldier did so long for another look at the pretty Princess; and so up came the dog by night and took her and dashed off at full speed. But the old lady-in-waiting put on her overboots

and ran just as fast after them, and when she saw them disappear into a big house she thought to herself, "Now I know where it is," and chalked up a big cross on the door. Then she went home to bed, and the dog came back too with the Princess. But when it saw a cross had been chalked on the door where the soldier was living, the dog also took a bit of chalk and put a

cross on every door in the town. That was a clever idea, because now, you see, the lady-in-waiting couldn't find the right door, as there were crosses on the whole lot of them.

Early in the morning the King and Queen, the old lady-in-waiting and all the Court officials sallied forth in order to see where it was the Princess had been.

"Here's the house!" said the King, when he saw the first door with a cross on it.

"No, it's there, darling!" said the Queen, catching sight of the second door with a cross on it.

"But here's another – and there's another!" they all kept saying. Whichever way they turned, there were crosses on the doors. So then they soon realized that it was no good searching any longer.

But the Queen, you know, was a very clever woman, who could do more than just drive out in a coach. She took her great golden scissors and cut up a large piece of silk and sewed the pieces together into a pretty little bag, which she filled with the finest buckwheat flour. She fastened the little bag to the Princess' back, and then she snipped a little hole in the bag, so as to sprinkle the flour wherever the Princess went. At night, up came the dog once more, took the Princess on his back and ran off with her to the soldier, who loved her so dearly and did so wish he were a prince and could marry her.

The dog never noticed how the flour kept leaking out all the way from the castle to the soldiers' window, where it ran up the wall with the Princess. The next morning it was quite plain to the King and Queen where their daughter had been going; so they took the soldier and put him in prison.

There he sat. Ugh! how dark and dreary his cell was! And, beside, they kept saying to him "To-morrow you're going to be hanged!" That didn't sound at all cheerful, and the worst of it was he had left his tinder-box at the inn. In the morning, through the iron bars of his little window, he watched people hurrying out of the town to see him hanged. He heard the drums and saw the soldiers marching past. Everyone was afoot. Among them was a cobbler's boy in leather apron and slippers; he was trotting along so fast that one of his slippers came off and flew right against the wall where the soldier sat peeping out between the iron bars.

"I say! you young cobbler, you don't need to hurry like that," the soldier said to him, "They can't begin without me. But look here – if you will kindly run along to where I've been living and fetch me my tinder-box; you shall have twopence for your trouble; but mind you get a move on!" The cobbler's boy was very glad to earn twopence, so he sprinted off for the tinder-box, brought it to the soldier, and – well, now listen to what happened!

Outside the town a high gallows had been built, and round about it stood the soldiers and thousands and thousands of people. The King and Queen sat on a beautiful throne opposite the judge and all his councillors.

Already the soldier had climbed the ladder; but just as they were going to put the rope round his neck he reminded them that, before being executed, a criminal always had the right to ask for one harmless favour. He said he would so like to smoke a pipe of tobacco – after all, it would be the last pipe he could smoke in this world.

Now, the King didn't like to say no to that; so the soldier took his tinder-box and struck a light – one, two, three! – and there stood all three dogs: the one with eyes as big as tea-cups, the one with eyes like mill-wheels, and the one which had eyes as big as the Round Tower.

"Save me now from being hanged!" said the soldier; and then the dogs flew at the judges and all the councillors, and seized some by their legs and others by their noses, and tossed them so high into the air that when they came down they were dashed to pieces.

"I won't be tossed!" said the King; but the biggest dog picked them both up, King and Queen, and sent them hurtling after the others. Then the soldiers got frightened, and the people all shouted out "Soldier boy, you shall be our King and have the pretty Princess." And they put the soldier in to the King's coach, and all three dogs went dancing in front of it and cried out "Hurrah!" And the boys whistled on their fingers, and the soldiers presented arms. The Princess came out of the copper castle and was made Queen, and how pleased she was! The wedding-feast lasted for a week, and the dogs sat at table with everyone else and kept rolling their great big eyes.

THE SNOW MAN

"*O*oh! I'm creaking all over in this lovely cold weather," said the snow man. I must say the wind knows how to sting life into you. And that goggle-eye over there – how she does stare!" – it was the sun he meant, which was just going down – "she won't get me to wince; I can hold on to my bits all right." These were two large three-cornered bits of roof-tiles that he had for eyes; the mouth was part of an old rake, and so he had teeth.

He had been born amid shouts of glee from the boys, and saluted with jingling of bells and cracking of whips from the sledges.

The sun went down and the full moon rose, round and huge, clear and lovely in the blue sky. "There she comes again from another direction," said the snow man. He imagined it was the sun appearing once more. "I have cured her of staring. Now she can hang there and light me up to see myself. If I only knew how one sets about moving! I should so like to move. If I could, I would go straight away and do some sliding on the ice, as I saw the boys doing. But I don't know how to run."

"Be-off-off!" barked the old watchdog from his chain. He was a bit husky; he had been like that ever since he had lived indoors and lay close to the fire. "The sun will teach you to run all right! I saw that happen last year to the snow man before you, to the one before him, 'be-off-off' – and off they've gone."

"I don't follow you, mate," said the snow man. "Will that creature up there teach me how to run?" (He was referring to the moon.) "Well, yes, she ran fast enough just now, when I stared back at her; now she's creeping up from another direction."

"You don't know a thing," said the watchdog; "but, there, they've only just stuck you up. What you're looking at is called the moon; the other, who disappeared, was the sun. She'll come back tomorrow and show you well enough how to run – right down into the pond. There'll soon be a change in the weather, I can feel it in my left hind leg – such twinges! yes, the weather's going to change."

"I can't make him out," said the snow man, "though I've a feeling that it's something impleasant he's getting at. The one who stared and went down – he calls her the sun – she isn't my friend either, I feel sure of that."

"Be-off-off!" barked the watchdog, turned round three times about himself and lay down inside his kennel to sleep.

There really was a change in the weather. A thick clammy fog settled down in the early morning over the whole neighbourhood. At break of day there was a light breeze; the wind was so icy cold that the frost got a firm grip. But what a sight there was when the sun rose! All the trees and bushes were covered with hoar-frost; it was like a whole forest of white coral; it was as if all the boughs had been smothered with glittering white blossoms. Thousands of delicate twigs, that in summer are not to be seen because of all the leaves, now stood out, every one of them. It all looked just like lace and so dazzling white that a white radiance appeared to stream from every branch. The weeping birch stirred in the breeze, with life in it you might see in a tree in summer. You never saw such loveliness; and as the sun shone out, goodness! how everything sparkled as if it had been sprinkled over with diamond dust, and the whole snow-covered earth was a glitter of big diamonds – or you might also, suppose they were thousands of tiny candles, even whiter than the snow itself.

"How perfectly beautiful!" said a girl, as she stepped with a young man out into the garden and paused alongside the snow man, looking at the glistening trees. "You couldn't see anything lovelier even in summer," she said with sparkling eyes.

"Nor a fellow like this one here – you'd never come across him," said the young man and pointed at the snow man. "He's splendid!"

The girl laughed and gave the snow man a nod; then she tripped off with her friend across the snow, which crunched under them as if they were walking on starch.

"Who were those two?" the snow man asked the watchdog. "You've been here longer than I have; do you know them?"

"Indeed I do," replied the watchdog. "She sometimes pats my back, and he has given me a bone. I'll never bite *them.*"

"But what are they doing here?" asked the snow man.

"They're swee-eethearts! " said the watchdog. "They are to move in to a kennel of their own and gnaw bones together. Be-off-off!"

"Are these two just as important as you and I?" asked the snow man.

"Well, you see, they belong to the family," said the watchdog. "It's true, no one can be expected to know much if he was born yesterday. That's clearly the case with you. Now, I possess age and knowledge; I know everyone here at the house. There was a time when I didn't have to stand chained up here in the cold. Be-off-off!"

"But cold is delightful," said the snow man. "Do go on with your story! But don't keep rattling your chain; that upsets me."

"Be-off-off!" barked the watchdog. "I was a puppy then; a sweet little thing, they said I was. There I lay indoors on a velvet chair, curled up on my lady's lap. I was kissed on the nose and had my paws wiped with an embroidered handkerchief; they called me "the beautifullest", "ducky-ducky-darling" ... But soon I grew too big for them, and they gave me to the housekeeper. I came down to the basement; you can see into it from where you're standing. You can see down into the room where I was lord and master, for that's what I was with the housekeeper. I dare say they were hurribler quarters than upstairs, but it was more comfortable here: I wasn't pawed and lugged about by children as I had been upstairs. I got just as good food as before, and much more of it. I had my own cushion, and then there was a stove. That's the most glorious thing in the world at this time of the year. I used to crawl right in underneath it, till I was out of sight. Oh, I still dream of that stove. Be-off-off!"

"Is a stove really so nice to look at?" asked the snow man. "Is it at all like me?"

" It's just the opposite of you. Coal-black, and has a long neck with brass collar. It feeds on logs, so that flames shoot out of its mouth. You can keep beside it, close up, or right under; it is such a comfort. You must be able to see it through the window from where you are."

And the snow man looked and, sure enough, he saw a shiny blackpolished object with a brass collar; fire was gleaming out from below. The snow man had a strange sensation, a feeling he couldn't himself account for. Something came over him that was quite new to him, though people all know it who are not snow men.

"And why did you leave her?" asked the snow man, for he felt that the stove must be one of the female sex. "How could you desert such a spot?"

"Well, the fact is I had to," said the watchdog. "They turned me out and chained me up here. I had bitten the youngest son of the house in the leg, because he had kicked away the

bone I was gnawing; a bone for a bone, I thought. But they didn't like it, and from that day I've been chained up and have lost my clear voice; listen how hoarse I am – be-off-off! That was the end of it all."

The snow man gave up listening. He still went on staring into the housekeeper's basement, down into her room where the stove stood on its four iron legs and looked about the size of the snow man himself.

"There's a queer creaking inside me," he said. "Am I never to come into that room? It's an innocent wish, and surely our innocent wishes ought to be granted. It's my greatest wish, my one and only wish; and it would be hardly fair if it weren't satisfied. I must come in, I must nestle up against her, even if I have to smash the window."

"You'll never come in there," said the watchclog; and if you did reach the stove you'd soon be off, off!"

"I'm as good as off already," said the snow man. "I feel I'm breaking up."

All day long the snow man stood looking in at the window. At dusk the room became still more inviting. The stove shone so kindly in a way that neither moon nor sun can ever shine – no, but as only a stove can shine, when there's something in it. When the door was opened, the flame shot out; that was its habit. The snow man's white face went flaming red, and the pink glow spread right up his chest.

"It's more than I can bear," he said. "How pretty she looks when she puts out her tongue!"

The night was very long, but not for the snow man. He stood there with his own beautiful thoughts, and they froze till they crackled. In the early morning the basement windows were frozen over; they had the loveliest ice-ferns any snow man could ask for, but they hid the stove. The panes refused to thaw, so he couldn't see her. There was crackling and crunching, it was exactly the kind of frosty weather to delight a snow man; but he was not delighted. He might and ought to have felt so happy, but he wasn't happy; he had 'stove-sickness'.

"That's a serious complaint for a snow man," said the watchdog, "I've had it myself, but I've got over it – be-off-off! There's a change in the weather coming."

And there was a change in the weather; it turned to a thaw. The thaw increased, the snow man decreased. He didn't say anything, he didn't complain, and that's a sure sign.

One morning he collapsed. Where he had been standing there was something like a broom-handle sticking out; it was round this the boys had built him up.

"Now I understand about his 'stove-sickness'," said the watchdog. "The snow man has a stove-rake in his body; that's what upset him, and now he's done with it. Be-off-off!"

And soon winter was done with too.

"Be-off-off!" barked the watchdog; but the little girls at the house sang:

"Sweet woodruff, now's the time to sprout.
and, willow, hang your mittens out.
Come, lark, and cuckoo, when you sing
then winter's gone and here is spring.
I'll join you both – twit-twit! cuckoo!
Come, darling sun, we long for you!"

After that, nobody gave a thought to the snow man.

THE FIR TREE

Out in the wood was a fir tree, such a pretty little fir tree. It had a good place to grow in and all the air and sunshine it wanted, while all around it were numbers of bigger comrades, both firs and pines. But the little fir tree was in such a passionate hurry to grow. It paid no heed to the warmth of the sun or the sweetness of the air, and it took no notice of the village children who went chattering along when they were out after strawberries or raspberries; sometimes they came there with a whole jugful or had got strawberries threaded on a straw, and then they sat down by the little tree and said, "Oh, what a dear little tree!" That was not at all the kind of thing the tree wanted to hear.

The next year it had shot up a good deal, and the year after that its girth had grown even bigger; for, with a fir tree, you can always tell how old it is by the number of rings it has.

"Oh, if only I were a tall tree like the others," sighed the little fir. "Then I'd be able to spread out my branches all round me and see out over the wide world with my top. The birds would come and nest in my branches and, whenever it was windy, I'd be able to nod just as grandly as the others."

It took no pleasure in the sunshine or the birds or the pink clouds that, morning and evening, went sailing overhead.

When winter came and the snow lay sparkling white all around, then a hare would often come bounding along and jump right over the little tree – oh, how annoying that was! ... But two winters passed and by the third winter the tree had grown so tall that the hare had to run round it. Yes, grow, grow become tall and old – that was much the finest thing in the world, thought the tree.

In the autumn the woodcutters always came and felled some of the tallest trees. That used to happen every year; and the young fir which was now quite a sizable tree, trembled at the sight, for the splendid great trees would crack and crash to the ground; their branches were lopped off, and they looked all naked and spindly – they were hardly recognisable – and then they were loaded on to waggons and carted away by horses out of the wood.

Where were they off to? What was in store for them?

In the spring, when the swallow and the stork arrived, the tree asked them, "Do you know where they've gone – where they've been taken to? Have you seen anything of them?"

The swallows knew nothing, but the stork looked thoughtful and replied with a nod, "Yes, I believe I know. I came across a lot of new ships, as I flew here from Egypt; they had splendid masts – I daresay it was them – I could smell the fir, and they asked to be remembered to you. Oh, how straight they stand!"

"How I do wish that I were big enough to fly across the sea! And, as a matter of fact, what sort of a thing is this sea? What does it look like?"

"That would take far too long to explain," said the stork and went his way.

"Rejoice in your youth," said the suribeams; "rejoice in your lusty growth, and in the young life that is in you." And the wind kissed the tree, and the dew wept tears over it, but this meant nothing to the fir tree.

As Christmas drew near, quite young trees were cut down, trees that often were nothing like so big or so old as our fir tree, which knew no peace and was always longing to get away. These young trees – and they were just the very handsomest ones – always kept their branches; they were laid on waggons and carted away by horses out of the wood.

"Where are they off to?" asked the fir tree. "They are no bigger than I am; there was even one that was much smaller. Why did they all keep their branches? Where are they going?"

"We know, we know!" twittered the sparrows. "We've been peeping in at the windows down in the town; we know where they're going. All the glory and splendour you can imagine awaits them. We looked in through the window-panes and saw how the trees were planted in the middle of a cosy room and decorated with the loveliest things: gilded apples, honey cakes, toys and hundreds of candles."

"And then?" asked the fir tree, quivering in every branch. "And then? What happens then?"

"Well, we didn't see any more. But it was magnificent."

"I wonder if it will be my fate to go that dazzling road," cried the tree in delight. "It's even better than crossing the ocean. How I'm longing for Christmas! I'm now just as tall and spreading as the others who were taken away last year. Oh, if only I were already on the waggon – if only I were in the cosy room amidst all that glory and splendour! And then? yes, there must be something still better, still more beautiful in store for me – or why should they decorate me like that? – something much greater, and much more splendid. But what? Oh, the labouring and longing I go through! I don't know myself, what's the matter with me."

"Rejoice in me," said the air and the sunlight; "rejoice in your lusty youth out here in the open."

But the fir tree did nothing of the kind. It went on growing and growing; there it was, winter and summer, always green – dark green. People who saw it remarked, "That's a pretty tree"; and at Christmas time it was the first to be felled. The axe cut deep through pit and marrow, and the tree fell to the earth with a sigh, faint with pain, with no more thoughts of any happiness; it was so sad at parting from its home, from the place where it had grown up. For it knew that never again would it see those dear old friends, the little bushes and flowers that grew around – yes, and perhaps not even the birds. There was nothing pleasant about such a parting.

The tree didn't come to itself till it was being unloaded in the yard with the other trees and it heard a man say, "That one's a beauty – that's the one we'll have."

Now came two lackeys in full fig and carried the fir tree into a splendid great room. There were portraits all round on the walls, and by the big tile fireplace stood huge Chinese vases with lions on their lids. There were rocking-chairs, silk-covered sofas, large tables piled with picturebooks and toys worth hundreds of pounds – at least, so said the children.

And the fir tree was propped up in a great firkin barrel filled with sand, though no one could see it was a barrel because it was draped round with green baize and was standing on a gay-coloured carpet. How the tree trembled! Whatever was going to happen? Servants and young ladies alike were soon busy decorating it. On the branches they hung the little nets that

had been cut out of coloured paper, each net being filled with sweets; gilded apples and walnuts hung down as if they were growing there, and over a hundred red, blue and white candles were fastened to the branches. Dolls that looked just like living people – such as the tree had never seen before – hovered among the greenery, while right up at the very top they had put a great star of gold tinsel; it was magnificent – you never saw anything like it.

"Tonight," they all said, "tonight it's going to sparkle – you see!"

"Oh, if only tonight were here!" thought the tree. "If only the candles were already lighted! What happens then, I wonder? Do trees come from the wood to look at me? Will the sparrows fly to the window-panes? Shall I take root here and keep my decorations winter and summer?"

Well, well, – a nice lot the fir tree knew! But it had got barkache from sheer longing, and barkache is just as bad for a tree as headache is for the rest of us.

At last the candles were lighted – what a blaze, what magnificence! It made the tree tremble in every branch, until one of the candles set fire to the greenery – didn't that smart!

"Oh dear!" cried the young ladies and quickly put out the fire. It was so afraid of losing any of its finery, and it felt quite dazed by all that magnificence ... Then suddenly both folding doors flew open, and a flock of children came tearing in, as if they were going to upset the whole tree. The older people followed soberly behind; the little ones stood quite silent – but only for a moment – then they made the air ring with their shouts of delight. They danced round the tree, and one present after another was pulled off it.

"Whatever are they doing?" thought the tree. "What's going to happen?" The candles burned right down to their branches and, as they did so, they were put out, and the children were allowed to plunder the tree. They rushed in at it, till it creaked in every branch; if it hadn't been fastened to the ceiling by the top and the gold star, it would have tumbled right over.

The children danced round with their splendid toys, and nobody looked at the tree except the old nurse, who went peering among the branches – though this was only to see if there wasn't some fig or apple that had been overlooked.

"A story – tell us a story!" cried the children, dragging a little fat man over towards the tree. He sat down right under it, "for then we are in the greenwood," he said, "and it will be so good for the tree to listen with you. But I'll only tell one story. Would you like the one about *Hickory-Dickory* or the one about *Humpty-Dumpty, who fell downstairs and yet came to the throne and married the Princess?*"

"*Hickory-Dickory*", cried some; *"Hump-ty-Dumpty,"* cried others. There was such yelling and shouting; only the fir tree was quite silent and thought "Shan't I be in it as well? Isn't there anything for me to do?" But of course, it *had* been in it – done just what it had to do.

The little fat man told them the story of *Humpty-Dumpty, who fell downstairs and yet came to the throne and married the Princess.* And the children clapped their hands and called out, "Tell us another story! One more!" They wanted to have *Hickory-Dickory* as well, but they only got the one about *Humpty-Dumpty.*

The fir tree stood there in silent thought: never had the birds out in the wood told a story like that. "Humpty-Dumpty fell downstairs and yet married the Princess – well, well, that's how they go on in the great world!" thought the fir tree, and felt it must all be true, because the story-teller was such a nice man. "Well, who knows? Maybe I too shall fall downstairs and marry a Princess." And it looked forward to being decked out again next day with candles and toys, tinsel and fruit.

"I shan't tremble tomorrow," it thought. "I mean to enjoy my magnificence to the full. Tomorrow I shall again hear the story about Humpty-Dumpty and perhaps the one about Hickory-Dickory as well." And the tree stood the whole night in silent thought.

The next morning in came manservant and maid.

"Now all the doings will begin again," thought the tree. Instead, they hauled it out of the room, up the stairs and into the attic, where they stowed it away in a dark corner out of the daylight. "What's the meaning of this?" wondered the tree. "What is there for me to do here?

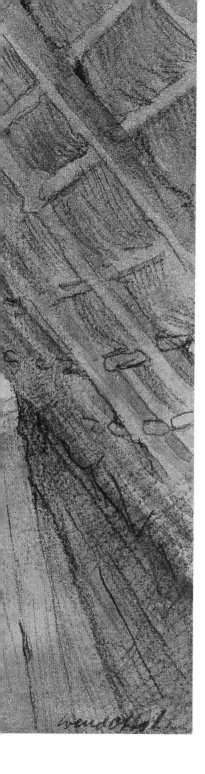

What am I to listen to?" And it leaned up against the wall and stood there thinking and thinking ... It had plenty of time for that, because days and nights went by. No one came up there and when at last somebody did come it was to put some big boxes away in the corner; the tree was completely hidden – you might have thought it was utterly forgotten.

"It's winter by now outside," thought the tree. "The ground will be hard and covered with snow, people wouldn't be able to plant me; so I expect I shall have to shelter here till the spring. How considerate! How kind people are! ... If only it weren't so dark and so terribly lonely in here! Not even a little hare ... It was so jolly out in the wood, when the snow was lying and the hare went bounding past; yes, even when it jumped right over me, though I didn't like it at the time. Up here it's too lonely for words."

"Pee-pee!" squeaked a little mouse just then, creeping out on the floor; and another one followed it. They sniffed at the fir tree and slipped in and out of its branches. "It's horribly cold," said the little mice, "though this is actually a splendid place to be in, don't you think, old fir tree?"

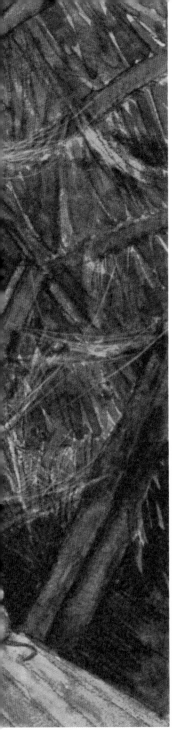

"I'm not a bit old," answered the fir tree. "There are lots of people who are much older than I am."

"Where do you hail from?" asked the mice, "and what do you know?" (They were being dreadfully inquisitive). "Do tell us about the loveliest place on earth. Have you ever been there? Have you been in the larder, where there are cheeses on the shelves and hams hanging from the ceiling – where you can dance on tallow candles and you go in thin and come out fat?"

"No. I don't know the larder," said the tree, "but I know the wood, where the sun shines and the birds sing;" and then it told all about the days when it was young. The little mice had never heard anything like it before, and they listened closely and said, "Why, what a lot you've seen! How happy you must have been!"

"I?" said the fir tree and pondered over what it had just been saying, "yes, they were really very pleasant times." But then it went on to tell them about Christmas Eve, when it had been tricked out with cakes and candles.

"Ooh!" said the little mice, "you *have* been a happy old fir tree."

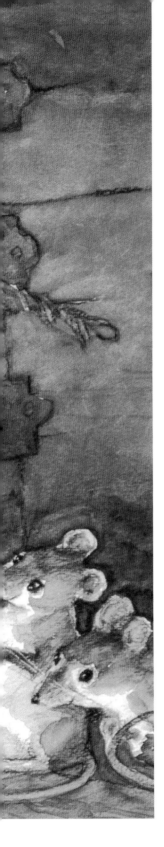

"I'm not a bit old," repeated the tree; "I've only this winter come from the wood. I'm just in my prime; my growth is only being checked for a while."

"What lovely stories you tell!" said the little mice; and they came back the following night with four more little mice who wanted to hear the tree tell stories, and the more it told the better it remembered everything itself, thinking, "Those were really rather jolly times. But they may come again, they may come again. Humpty-Dumpty fell downstairs and yet won the Princess; perhaps I too may win a Princess." And then the fir tree suddenly remembered such a sweet little birch tree growing out in the wood; that, for the fir tree, would be a real beautiful Princess:

"Who is Humpty-Dumpty?" asked the little mice. Then the fir tree told them the whole fairy tale; it could remember every word; and the little mice were ready to jump up to the top of the tree for sheer enjoyment. The night after, many more mice turned up and, on the Sunday, even two rats. But these declared that the tale was not at all amusing, which disappointed the little mice because now they didn't think so much of it either.

"Is that the only story you know?" asked the rats.

"Only that one," replied the tree. "I heard it on the happiest evening of my life, but I never realised then how happy I was."

"It's a fearfully dull story. Don't you know any about pork and tallow candles? One about the larder?"

"No," said the tree.

"Well, then, thank you for nothing" answered the rats and went home again.

In the end, the little mice kept away as well, and the tree said with a sigh, "It really was rather nice with them sitting round me, those eager little mice, listening to what I told them. Now that's over too ... though I shall remember to enjoy myself, when I'm taken out once more."

But when would that happen? Well, it happened one morning when people came up and rummaged about the attic. The boxes were being moved, and the tree was dragged out. They certainly dumped it rather hard on to the floor, but one of the men at once pulled it along towards the stairs where there was daylight.

"Life's beginning again for me!" thought the tree. It could feel the fresh air, the first sunbeams – and now it was out in the courtyard. Everything happened so quickly that the tree quite forgot to look at itself, there was so much to see all around. The yard gave on to a garden where everything was in bloom. The roses smelt so sweet and fresh as they hung over the little trellis, the lime trees were blossoming, and the swallows flew around saying, "Kvirra-virra-veet, my husband's arrived!" But it wasn't the fir tree they were thinking of.

"This is the life for me!" it cried out joyfully, spreading out its branches. Alas! they were all withered and yellow, and the tree lay in a corner among weeds and nettles. The gold-paper star was still in its place at the top and glittered away in the bright sunshine.

Playing in the courtyard itself were a few of the merry children who at Christmas time had danced round the tree and were so pleased with it. One of the smallest ran up and tore off the gold star.

"Look what I've found still there on that nasty old Christmas tree!" he said, trampling on the branches so that they crackled under his boots.

And the tree looked at the fresh beauty of the flowers in the garden, and then at itself, and it wished it had stayed in that dark corner up in the attic. It thought of the fresh days of its youth in the wood, of that merry Christmas Eve, and of the little mice who had listened with such delight to the story of Humpty-Dumpty.

"All over!" said the poor tree, "if only I had been happy while I could! All over!"

And the man came and chopped up the tree into small pieces, till there was quite a heap. It made a fine blaze under the big copper; and the tree groaned so loudly that every groan was like a little shot going off. This made the children who were playing run in and sit down before the fire; and as they looked into it they shouted "bang!" – but at every pop (which was a deep groan) the tree thought of a summer's day in the wood, or of a winter's night out there when the stars were shining; it thought of Christmas Eve and of *Humpty-Dumpty*, the only fairy tale it had ever heard and was able to tell ... And by this time the tree was burnt right up.

The boys were playing in the yard, and the smallest of them had on his chest the gold star which had crowned the tree on its happiest evening. That was all over now, and it was all over with the tree, and so it is with the story. That's what happens at last to every story – all over, all over!

SIMPLE SIMON

*A*way in the country, in an old manorhouse, lived an old squire. He had two sons who were so clever that – well, the fact is they were too clever by half. They made up their minds to go and propose to the King's daughter; and they had a perfect right to do this, because she had announced that she would marry the man who she thought was best able to speak up for himself.

The two sons now spent a week in preparation. A week was all they were allowed; but it was quite long enough, for they had had a good education, and that is such a help. One of them knew the whole Latin dictionary off by heart, and also the local newspaper for the last three years, both backwards and forwards. The other son had learnt up all the by-laws of the city companies and the things every alderman is supposed to know; he thought this would help him to talk politics with the Princess; and, besides, he knew how to embroider braces, he was so very clever with his fingers.

"I shall win the Princess!" cried both of them; and so their father gave them each a beautiful horse. The brother who had learnt off the dictionary and the newspapers got a coal-black horse; and the one who knew all about aldermen and could do embroidery got a milk-white horse; and then they smeared the corners of their mouths with cod-liver oil, so that the words would come out pat. All the servants were down in the courtyard to see them mount their horses, when just at that moment up came the third brother; for there were three of them, though nobody ever took count of the third, because he wasn't a scholar like the other two. They called him Simple Simon.

"Where are you two off to in that get up?" he asked.

"We're going to Court, to talk our way into favour with the Princess. Haven't you heard the proclamation that's been read out all over the country?" And then they told him all about it.

"Gosh! I mustn't miss this!" said Simple Simon. But his brothers laughed at him and rode away.

"Dad, let me have a horse!" cried Simple Simon. "I do so feel like getting married. If she'll have me, she'll have me; and if she won't, then I'll marry her all the same."

"What nonsense!" said the father. "I've no horse for you. Why, you never open your mouth. But look at your brothers – they are splendid fellows."

"If I can't have a horse," said the boy, "then I'll ride the billy-goat. It's my own, and it'll carry me all right, I know." Then he got astride the billy-goat, dug his heels into its sides and dashed off down the road. Phew! What a rate they went! "Look out! Here we come!" yelled Simple Simon, and his cries went echoing after him.

But his brothers rode on ahead in complete silence. They never said a word, because they had to turn over in their minds all the clever remarks they were going to make. It had to be most cunningly worked out, I can tell you.

"Tally-ho!" shouted Simple Simon, "here we are! Look what I found on the road," and he showed them a dead crow he had picked up.

"You simpleton!" they said. "What are you going to do with that?"

"I shall give it to the Princess."

"Yes, do!" they answered, laughing as they rode on.

"Tally-ho! Here we are! Now look what I've found. You don't find that on the road every day."

The brothers turned round again to see what it was. "You simpleton!" they said. "Why, that's an old clog with the vamp missing. Is the Princess to have that as well?"

"Yes, of course," said Simple Simon; and his brothers only laughed at him and rode on till they were a long way ahead.

"Tally-ho! Here we are!" shouted Simon. "My word! This is getting better and better. Tally-ho! This is grand!"

"What have you found this time?" asked the brothers.

"Oh, it's too good for anything," said Simple Simon. "Won't she be pleased, the Princess!"

"Ugh!" said the brothers. "Why, it's mud straight out of the ditch."

"Yes, that's just what it is," said Simple Simon, "and the very finest sort, too; it slips right through your fingers." And he filled his pocket with the mud.

But his two brothers rode on as hard as they could go, and the result was that they drew up at the city gate a whole hour ahead of him and found the suitors being given numbers in the order of their arrival. They were made to stand in rows, six in each file, and so close together that they couldn't move their arms. This was just as well, for otherwise they might have stabbed each other in the back, just because one was in front of the other.

The rest of the inhabitants all crowded round the castle, right up against the windows, so as to watch the Princess receiving her suitors; but as soon as ever one of them came into her presence, he was completely tongue-tied. "No good!" the Princess kept saying. "Skedaddle!"

Now it was the turn of the brother who knew the dictionary by heart. But he had clean forgotten it while he was standing in the queue; and the floor creaked under him, and the ceiling was all covered with mirrors, so that he saw himself standing on his head. At the window stood three clerks and an alderman, who all wrote down every word that was spoken, so that it could go straight into the newspaper and be sold for a penny at the street-corner. It was dreadful: and what's more, they had made up such a fire that the stove was red-hot.

"It's very warm in here," said the suitor.

"That's because my father's roasting cockerels to-day," said the Princess.

"O-o-oh!" was all he could say, as he stood there. He hadn't expected a remark like that, and he was hoping to say something witty. "O-o-oh!"

"No good!" said the Princess. "Skedaddle!" – and away he had to go. After that the second brother came in.

"It's dreadfully hot in here," he said.

"Yes, we're roasting cockerels for dinner," said the Princess.

"I b-beg your – b-beg your – " he stuttered; and the clerks all wrote down "I b-beg your – b-beg your –"

"No good!" said the Princess. "Skedaddle!"

Now it was Simple Simon's turn. He came trotting in on the billygoat, right into the palace-room. "Why, it's as hot as blazes in here!" he said.

"That's because I'm roasting cockerels," said the Princess.

"Oh, I say, that's lucky," said Simple Simon. "So I suppose I can have a crow roasted, can't I!"

"Of course you can, quite easily," said the Princess; "but have you got anything to roast it in, for I've neither pot nor pan."

"But I have," said Simon. "Here's a cooker with a tin handle!" And he produced the old clog and popped the crow straight into it.

"It will make quite a meal," said the Princess. "But what shall we do for gravy?"

"I've got that in my pocket," said Simon. "I've enough and to spare." And he tipped a little mud out of his pocket.

"I do like that!" said the Princess. "You know how to answer; you can speak up for yourself, and you're the one I'm going to marry! But do you realize that every word we've been saying has been written down and will be in the papers to-morrow? Look there by the window – three clerks and an old alderman; and the alderman is the worst, because he doesn't understand a thing." Of course she said this just to frighten him. And the clerks all guffawed and made a great blot of ink on the floor.

"So these are the gentry?" said Simon. "Well, here's one for the alderman!" And he turned out his pocket and let him have the mud full in the face.

"Well done!" cried the Princess. "I could never have done that, but I'll soon learn." So in the end Simple Simon became King with a wife of his own and a crown and a throne. And all this comes straight out of the alderman's newspaper; so it may not be perfectly true!

THE WILD SWANS

$\mathcal{F}$ar, far away, where the swans fly to when we are having winter, lived a King who had eleven sons and one daughter, Elise. The eleven brothers – they were Princes – went to school with stars on their breasts and swords at their sides. They wrote on gold slates with diamond pencils, and they were just as good at learning their lessons off by heart as at reading them from the book; you could tell at once they were Princes. Their sister Elise sat on a little plate-glass stool with a picture-book that had cost half the kingdom. Yes, those children had all they wanted, but that wasn't to go on for ever.

Their father, who reigned over the whole country, married a wicked Queen who was not at all nice to the poor children – they noticed it the very first day. There was a great set-out for the wedding all over the Castle, and so the children were left to play "visitors". But instead of them getting their usual fill of cakes and roast apples, the Queen only gave them sand in a teacup and told them they could just pretend it was something.

A week later she sent the little sister, Elise, out into the country to be boarded with some farm-people, and it wasn't long before she put so many ideas into the King's head about the poor Princes that he ended by never giving them a thought.

"Fly out into the world and look after yourselves," said the wicked Queen. "Fly in the form of big birds without voices." But all the same she couldn't harm them as much as she would have liked to; they were turned into eleven beautiful wild swans. With a strange cry they flew out of the castle windows away over the park and the woods.

lt was still early morning when they passed the spot where their sister Elise lay sleeping in the farm-house. They hovered above her roof, twisted their long necks and beat their wings; but no one heard them or saw them. They had to fly off again, high up into the clouds, far out into the wide world. At last they came to a big dark wood that stretched right down to the shore.

Poor little Elise was left in the farm-house to play with a green leaf; she had nothing else to play with. She pricked a hole in the leaf and peeped up at the sun through it and this made her think she could see the bright eyes of her brothers, and whenever the warm rays of the sun shone on her cheeks it reminded her of all their kisses.

One day passed just like another. When the wind blew through the big rose bushes in front of the house, it whispered to the roses, "Can anyone be prettier than you?" And the roses nodded their heads – "Yes, Elise is." And when the old wife sat on Sundays at the door reading her hymn-book, the wind used to turn over the pages and say to the book, "Can anyone be more devout than you?" "Yes, Elise is," answered the hymn-book. And that was perfectly true, what the roses and the hymn-book said.

When she was fifteen, she had to go back home; and when the Queen saw how pretty she was, it made her angry and full of hatred. She would have liked to turn her into a wild swan like her brothers, but she didn't dare to straight away because the King wanted to see his daughter.

Early in the morning the Queen went to the bathroom, which was built of marble and decked out with soft cushions and the most beautiful rugs, and she took three toads, kissed them, and said to the first one, "Sit on Elise's head when she gets into the bath, so that she becomes as lazy as you." To the second one the Queen said, "Sit on her forehead, so that she may become as ugly as you and her father won't know her." "And you'" she whispered to the third toad, "keep close to her heart and give her wicked thoughts to torture her." Then she put the toads into the clear water, which at once turned a greenish colour, and she called Elise, undressed her and made her go into the water. As she plunged in, one toad hopped into her hair, another on to her forehead, and the third on to her breast; but Elise didn't seem to notice anything. Directly she stood up, there were three poppies floating on the water. If the creatures hadn't been poisonous and kissed by the witch, they would have been turned into red roses; though, mind you, they did change into flowers, just from resting on her head and at her heart. She was too innocent and good for witchcraft to have any power over her.

When the wicked Queen saw this, she rubbed walnut-juice into her till she was quite dark-brown; she smered her pretty face with a nasty smelly ointment, and let her beautiful hair get all matted. You would never have known it was the pretty Elise.

So when her father saw her, he was horrified and said that this wasn't his daughter. Nor could anyone else recognize her; no one could but the watch-dog and the swallows, and they were small fry whose opinion went for nothing.

Poor Elise cried, and her thoughts turned to her eleven brothers who had all disappeared. Sadly she crept out of the Castle and walked all day across field and fen till she came to the big wood. She had no idea where to make for, but she felt so glum and missed her brothers terribly. They, too, no doubt, like herself, were roving about somewhere; she would look for them and find them.

She had not been long in the wood when night fell. She had wandered far away from any road or path; and now she lay down on the soft moss, said her evening prayer, and rested her head on a tree-stump. The air was very soft and still, and all around in the grass and on the moss were ever so many glow-worms shining like green fire. When she gently touched one of the boughs with her hand, the gleaming insects fell about her like shooting stars.

All night she dreamt about her brothers; they were playing together as children again, writing on gold slates with diamond pencils, and looking at the lovely picture-book that had cost half a kingdom – though on the slate they no longer wrote simply noughts and crosses. No, they wrote down the bold deeds they had accomplished, all they had been through and had seen. And in the picturebook everything was alive; the birds sang, people came out of the book and talked to Elise and her brothers. But when she turned the page they at once jumped in again, so as not to make a muddle of the pictures.

When she woke up, the sun was alreday high; in fact, she couldn't really see it because the tall trees spread out their branches so thickly overhead – though the golden sunbeams played through them like fluttering gauze. There was a fresh smell of greenery, and the birds almost came and perched on her shoulders. She heard the plashing of water; there were a number of large springs that all flowed into a pond with a fine sandy bottom to it. And although there were thick bushes growing round it, there was one place where the stags had rooted out a great opening; and here Elise made her way down to the water, which was so clear that if the wind hadn't stirred the boughs and bushes she might have thought they were painted on the bottom of the pond – so sharply was every leaf reflected there, whether it had the sun shining through it or hung completely in the shade.

The moment she saw the reflection of her own face she was horrified, it was so brown and hideous; but when she dipped her hand in the water and rubbed eyes and forehead, the white skin shone out again. After that, she took off her clothes and waded out into the fresh water; nowhere in the world could there have been found a lovelier royal child than she was.

When she was dressed again and had plaited her long hair, she went to the bubbling spring, drank from her cupped hands, and then wandered further on into the wood without really kno-wing where she was going. She thought of her brothers, and of the good God who would certainly not forget her; it was he who made the wild apples grow food for the hungry, he who now showed her just such a tree, its branches weighed down with fruit. Here she ate her dinner, put props under the branches, and then walked on into the darkest portion of the wood. There all was so still that she could hear her own footsteps, hear every little withered leaf that was crumpled in her path. Not a bird was to be seen, not a ray of sun could pierce the dense foliage of the trees; the tall trunks stood so near to each other that, when she looked ahead, it was as though she were shut in by a whole lattice-work of timber, set close together. Oh, here was loneliness as she had never known it before.

The night grew very dark; not a single little glow-worm gave out its light from the moss. Sadly she lay down to sleep. Then it seemed to her that the branches overhead were parted and that God looked down on her with gentle eyes and that little angels were peeping out over his head

and under his arms. When she woke up in the morning, she wasn't sure whether she had dreamt it or whether it really happened.

She had only gone a short way when she met an old woman with berries in her basket; the old woman gave her a few. Elise asked if she hadn't seen eleven princes riding through the wood. "No," said the old woman, "but yesterday I saw eleven swans with gold crowns on their heads swimming down the river near here." And she took Elise a little further till they reached a slope. At the foot of this wound a stream; the trees on its banks stretched their long leafy boughs across to each other, and where their natural growth was not enough for them to meet, there they had wrenched their roots out of the earth and leaned across the water with their branches intertwined.

Elise said good-bye to the old woman and walked along the river till she came where it flowed out by the great open shore. The whole glorious ocean lay there before the young girl's eyes; but not a sail nor a boat of any kind was to be seen – how ever was she to get any further? She looked at the countless pebbles lying there on the beach, all of them round from the grinding of water. Glass, iron, stones – everything that was washed up had been shaped by the water, although this was far softer than her delicate hand. "It never tires of rolling, and in this way it can smooth down what is hard. I will be just as tireless. Thank you for your lesson, you clear rolling waves. One day – my heart tells me – you will carry me to my dear brothers."

On the washed-up seaweed lay eleven white swan-feathers, which she collected into a bunch. They had drops of water on them – whether from dew or from tears, one could not say. It was lonely on the shore, but she didn't mind that, for the sea was continually changing. Yes, in a few hours it might change more than the freshwater lakes did in a whole year. If a large black cloud appeared, it was as though the sea would say, "I, too, can look dark and threatening;" and then the wind got up and the waves showed the white of their eyes. But if the clouds shone pink and the wind was lulled, then the sea was like a rose-leaf; sometimes it was green, sometimes white. Yet, however quietly it rested, there was always a gentle movement along the shore; softly the water rose and fell, like the breast of a sleeping child.

As the sun was about to set, Elise saw eleven wild swans with gold crowns on their heads flying towards the land; they hovered in the air, one behind the other, looking like a long white ribbon. Elise clambered up the slope and hid behind a bush, while the swans came and settled near her flapping their great white wings.

Directly the sun had sunk below the horizon, the swans' feathers suddenly fell away from them, and there stood eleven handsome princes, Elise's brothers. She uttered a loud cry; for although they had changed a lot, she knew it was them – felt that it must be them, sprang into their arms

and called them by their names. And they were overjoyed when they saw and recognized their little sister, who had grown so tall and beautiful. They laughed and cried, and between them soon came to understand how wicked their stepmother had been to them all.

"As long as the sun's in the sky," said the eldest, "we brothers fly as wild swans; but when the sun goes down, we get back our human shape. So we always have to be careful at sunset to have ground under our feet; for, you see, if we were then flying up in the clouds we should, as human beings crash to our death down below. We don't live here. There's a country beyond the sea that's just as beautiful as this, but it's a long way there; we have to cross the great ocean, and there's no island on our way where we might pass the night – nothing but a lonely little rock sticking up in the middle of it all, just big enough for us to rest on side by side. If the sea gets up, then the spray dashes high above us; but, all the same, we thank God for that little rock. There we can pass the night in our human shape, or else we could never visit our dear mother country; for we need two of the longest days of the year for our flight. Only once a year are we allowed to visit our own home; eleven days are all we may stay, flying over this great wood, from which we can see the castle where we were born and where our father lives and can also see the high tower of the church where Mother is buried … Here we feel a kinship with trees and bushes; here the wild horses gallop, over the plain as we saw them in our childhood; here the carcoal-burrier sings the old songs we danced to as children; here is the land of our fathers, the place we feel drawn to, and here we have found you, our darling sister. For two days longer we may stay here, but then we must fly away across the sea to a glorious country, and yet it is not our own. How can we take you with us? We have neither ship nor boat."

"If only I could set you free!" she exclaimed. And they talked together nearly all night, with only two or three hours' sleep.

Elise was woken up by the sound of swans' wings whirring overhead. Her brothers were again transformed and were flying round in large circles; in the end they disappeared altogether – though one of them the youngest, stayed behind. The swan laid its head in her lap, and she stroked its white wings; they kept with each other all day. Towards evening the others came back and, as the sun went down, there they stood in human form.

"Tomorrow we fly away and dare not come back for a whole year, but we couldn't possibly leave you like this. Have you the courage to come with us? My arm is strong enough to carry you through the wood; then surely, between us, our wings must be strong enough to fly with you across the sea."

"Yes, take me with you," said Elise.

They spent the whole of that night making a net from the supple bark of the willow and the sturdy rushes, till it was really strong. Elise lay down on this and, as soon as the sun appeared and the brothers were changed into wild swans, they seized the net in their beaks and flew up high into the clouds with their dear sister, who was still asleep. The rays of the sun fell straight on her face, and so one of the swans flew above her head to shade her with its outstretched wings.

They were a long way from land when Elise woke up. She thought she was still dreaming, so strange did it seem to her to be carried through the air, high up over the sea. Beside her was a bough full of delicious ripe berries and a bunch of tasty roots, which the youngest of her brothers had gathered and put there for her. She gave him a grateful smile, for she knew that he was the one flying just above her head and shading her with his outstretched wings.

They were so high up that the first ship they saw below them looked like a white seagull floating on the water. Behind them was a great cloud – a huge mountain of a cloud – and against this Elise could see the shadow of herself and of the eleven swans, looking enormous as they flew there. Never before had she seen such a splendid picture; but as the sun rose higher and the cloud was left further behind them, the shadowy picture disappeared.

All day long the swans went whizzing through the air like arrows, and yet not so fast as before because now they had their sister to carry. A storm got up, and night was approaching. Elise was terrified to see the sun going down, and still there was no sign of the lonely rock in the ocean. She fancied the swans were quickening the beat of their wings. Oh, dear! It was her fault that they were not getting on fast enough. The moment the sun had set, they would be turned into human beings, crash into the sea and be drowned. Then she prayed to God from the bottom of her heart; but still she could see nothing of the rock. Black clouds came up, violent squalls heralded a gale; the clouds loomed in one threatening billowing mass like lead, as they surged along, with flash after flash of lightning.

Now the sun had sunk to the very edge of the ocean, and Elise's heart trembled. Then, all at once, the swans darted downwards – so quickly that she thought she was falling – but the next moment they were gliding smoothly again. The sun was half below the horizon. Then for the first time she caught sight of the little rock underneath her; it looked no bigger than a seal sticking up its head out of the water. The sun was sinking fast; now it was as small as a star. And then her foot touched solid ground, the sun went out like the last spark of a bit of burning paper, and there were her brothers standing arm in arm around her – though there was only just room for them and for her and no more. The sea dashed against the rock and drenched them like a shower of rain; the sky was one continual glimmer of flame with peal after peal of rolling thunder; but the

211

brothers and their sister held each other's hands and sang a hymn, which they found was a comfort and gave them courage.

The air at dawn was pure and still. As soon as the sun rose, the swans flew off with Elise from the islet. There was still a strong sea running; and, as they gained height, the white foam on the dark-green sea looked to them like millions of swans swimming on the water.

When the sun got up higher, Elise saw in front of her, half floating in the air, a mountainous country with masses of ice glittering on the rocky slopes, and in the middle of it all a palace that seemed to stretch for miles, with rows and rows of bold colonnades one above another, while down below were woods of waving palm trees and gorgeous flowers as large as mill-wheels. She asked whether that was the country they were making for, but the swans shook their heads, for what she saw was the lovely everchanging cloud-palace of the fairy Morgana; they would never dare to take a mortal in there. Elise stared across at it; then mountains, woods and palace all melted away and in their place were a score of stately churches, all just like each other, with high towers and pointed windows. She fancied she heard the sound of an organ, but it was the sea she could hear. By this time she was quite close to the churches, and then they were changed into an entire fleet sailing along beneath her. She looked down ... and it was nothing but a sea-mist scudding across the water. Yes, it was an everchanging scene that was spread before her; and at last she sighted the real country she was bound for. The beautiful blue mountains rose in front of her. Long before the sun went down, she was sitting on the mountain side before a large cave that was overgrown with delicate green creepers; they looked like embroidered curtains.

"Now let's see what you dream about here tonight," said the youngest brother, as he showed her where she was to sleep.

"If only I could dream how to set you all free!" she answered. And her mind could think of nothing else, and she prayed most earnestly to God to help her; yes, even in her sleep she went on praying. And it seemed to her that she flew high up through the air to Morgana's cloud-palace

and that the fairy came to welcome her, looking so beautiful and dazzling – and yet so like the old woman who gave her berries in the wood and told her about the swans with the gold crowns on their heads.

"Your brothers can be set free," said the fairy. "But have you enough courage and endurance? It's true the sea is softer than your delicate hands, and yet it can alter the shape of hard stones. But the sea doesn't feel the pain your fingers will feel; it has no heart, and will not suffer the fear and agony you must endure. Do you see this stinging nettle I've got in my hand? There are lots of this kind growing round the cave where you sleep. Only these nettles and the ones that come up on the graves in the churchyard are any use – remember that. They are the ones you must gather, though they will blister your skin. Crush the nettles with your feet, and you will be able to get flax. With this you must weave and hem eleven shirts of mail with long sleeves. Throw these over the eleven wild swans, and the spell will be broken. But one thing you must bear well in mind – that from the moment you start work, and all the time till it's finished, even if it takes years, you must never speak. The first word you utter will stab your brothers to the heart like a murderous dagger. Their lives will depend on your tongue. Whatever you do, remember this!"

So saying she touched Elise's hand with the nettle; it burnt like fire and woke her up. There was broad daylight, and close to where she had been sleeping lay a nettle like the one she had seen in her dream. She knelt down in thanks to God, and then she went out of the cave to begin her work ... With her delicate hands she took hold of the horrid nettles, which seared her like fire and burnt great blisters on her hands and arms. But she would readily put up with this, if only she could set her dear brothers free. She crushed every nettle with her bare feet, and then wove the green flax with it.

After sunset her brothers came to her and were dismayed to find her so silent. They thought it was some fresh piece of witchcraft of the wicked stepmother's; but when they saw Elise's hands, they realized what she was doing for their sake, and the youngest brother burst out crying; and wherever his tears fell her pain stopped and the burning blisters disappeared.

She spent the whole night working, for she could not rest till she had freed her beloved brothers. All the next day, while the swans were gone off, she sat there by herself, and yet never had the time flown so quickly. One shirt of mail was done already, and she was just beginning on the second.

Suddenly a hunting horn rang out among the hills. Elise grew very frightened. Nearer and nearer came the sound; she could hear the baying of hounds. In terror she made for the cave, tied into a bundle the nettles she had gathered and hackled, and sat down on it. Just then a big hound came bounding out of the bushes, and then another, and yet another. They kept barking loudly and

running to and fro. In a very short time the whole hunt was there outside the cave; handsomest of them all was the King of the land. He came forward to Elise; never had he seen a more beautiful girl.

"How came you here, you lovely child?" he asked. Elise shook her head, for she didn't dare to speak; the deliverance – the very lives of her brothers were at stake. And she hid her hands under her apron, so that the King shouldn't see how she had to suffer.

"Come with me," he said. "This is no place for you. If you are as good as you are beautiful, I will dress you in silk and velvet, put a gold crown on your head, and you shall make your home in my richest palace" – and then he lifted her on to his horse. She cried and wrung her hands, but the King said, "I want you to be happy, that's all. One day you will thank me." Then away he rode through the mountains, holding her in front of him on his horse, and the hunt came galloping after.

As the sun went down, there lay the magnificent capital with its churches and domes ahead of them; and the King took her into his palace, where great fountains were playing in the lofty marble halls and where walls and ceiling were gay with splendid paintings. But she had no eyes for any of this – hers were filled with tears and sorrow. She resigned herself to letting the woman dress her in royal clothes, plait pearls in her hair and draw elegant gloves over her blistered fingers.

As she stood there in all that splendour, her beauty was so dazzling that the courtiers bowed still deeper before her, and the King chose her to be his bride – although the Archbishop shook his head and whispered that this pretty creature from the woods was a witch, he felt certain, who had blinded their eyes and turned the King's head.

But the King wouldn't hear of it. He ordered the music to play, the rarest dishes to be brought

in, and the loveliest girls to dance for her; she was taken, too, through sweet-scented gardens into the grandest rooms. But still no smile played about her lips or from her eyes; sorrow, it seemed, was all she could ever be heir to. And now the King showed the way to a little room near by, where she was to sleep. It was decked out with costly green hangings, so that it looked very like the cave that she came from. On the floor lay the bundle of flax she had spun from the nettles, and from the ceiling hung the shirt of mail she had already finished. One of the huntsmen had brought all this along with him as a curiosity.

"Here you can dream that your're back in your old home," said the King. "Here is the work you were busy with. Now, with all your splendour around you, it may amuse you to call those days to mind."

When Elise saw these things that were so dear to her heart, a smile played about her lips and the blood came back to her cheeks at the thought of being able to save her brothers. She kissed the King's hand, and he pressed her to his heart and had the church bells rung to announce the wedding. The lovely dumb girl from the woods was to be Queen of the land.

But then the Archbishop whispered wicked words into the King's ear – though they didn't reach his heart, for the wedding was to take place. The Archbishop himself had to set the crown on her head, and out of sheer spite he pressed the narrow circlet down over her forehead, so that it hurt her; and yet a heavier ring lay round her heart – sorrow for her brothers – and she never noticed the bodily pain. Her mouth was dumb, for a single word would have meant the death of her brothers; but in her eyes there lay a deep affection for the noble handsome King who did everything to make her happy. Every day she grew more and more fond of him. If only she dared confide in him – tell him of her suffering! But no, dumb she must remain, dumb to the end of her task. And so she used to slip away from him at night, make her way into the little private room that was fitted out like the cave, and there she wove one shirt after another; but just as she was beginning on the seventh, she ran out of flax.

She knew that the right nettles were growing in the churchyard, but she must gather them herself. How was she to get there?

"Oh, what is the pain in my fingers compared with this agony in my heart!" she thought. "I must risk it. God will not forget me." Then, as fearful of heart as though she were on some wicked errand, she stole down into the garden in the dear moonlight, went through the long avenues out into the empty streets till she came to the churchyard. There she saw, sitting on one of the largest gravestones, a group of frightful-looking witches called Lamias. They were taking off their rags as if they meant to bathe, and then they clawed with their long skinny fingers in the new-

made graves, dragged out the corpses and ate their flesh. Elise had to pass close by them, and they fastened their horrible eyes on her; but she said a prayer, gathered the stinging nettles and carried them back to the palace.

Only one person had seen her – the Archbishop. He was still up, while the others were asleep; so, after all, he was right in what he suspected – everything was not as it should be with the Queen. She was a witch, and that was how she had taken in the King and all his people.

When the King came to confession, he told him what he had seen and what he feared; and as the cruel words came from his lips, the carved images of the saints shook their heads as if to say, "It isn't true; Elise is innocent!" But the Archbishop explained it in quite another way and made out that the saints were witnessing against her and that they shook their heads at her being so wicked. At that, two great tears ran down the King's cheeks, and his heart misgave him as he went back home. At night he pretended to be asleep, though he got no peaceful slumber, for he noticed how Elise used to steal out of bed, doing this regularly every night; and each time he went quietly after her and saw her disappear into her little private room.

Day by day his looks grew darker. Elise noticed this but couldn't make out why it was. It frightened her; and how heavy was her heart when she thought of her brothers! Her salt tears ran down on the royal purple velvet and lay there like sparkling diamonds, and everyone who saw the rich splendour of her robes wished they were Queen. Meanwhile Elise had all but ended her task; only one more shirt was to be made. But now there was no flax left, and not a single nettle. So once again – only this time would be the last – she must go and gather a few handfuls in the churchyard. She was terrified at the thought of this lonely journey and of the horrible Lamias, but her will was as firm as her trust in God.

Off she went, but the King and the Archbishop followed after. They saw her disappear through the iron gates into the churchyard and, as they came up to it, there were the Lamias sitting on the gravestone just as Elise had seen them. The King turned away, for he fancied he saw her among them – her whose head that very evening had rested against his heart.

"Let the people judge her," he said. And the people condemned her to be burnt at the stake. She was led away from the splendid royal halls to a dark damp cell, where the wind whistled in through the barred window. In place of velvet and silk they gave her the bundle of nettles she had gathered; she could lay her head on that. The coarse itching shirts of mail she had woven would do for a blanket to cover her ... But they couldn't have given her anything more precious. She set to work again, with a prayer to her God. The street boys outside sang jeering songs about her; not a soul had a kind word to comfort her.

Then, towards evening, close to the grating, she heard the whir of a swan's wings. It was the youngest of the brothers who had found his sister. She sobbed aloud with joy although she knew that the coming night might well be the last she had to live. Still, for all that, her task was nearly done and her brothers were with her.

The Archbishop came in to be with her during her last hour – he had promised the King to do that – but Elise shook her head and made signs for him to go. That night she must finish her task, or else everything would have been wasted – all the pain, the tears and the sleepless nights. The

Archbishop went off saying the cruellest things about her; but poor Elise knew she was innocent and went on with her work.

Little mice scampered about the floor, dragging the nettles to her feet to give some help, and a thrush perched on a window bar and sang all night as cheerfully as he could, to keep up her spirits.

It was still only twilight; the sun would not rise for another hour. And there stood the eleven brothers at the palace gate, demanding to be taken to the King. But this couldn'tbe done (was the answer they got) for it was still night, the King was asleep and mustn't be disturbed. They beg-

ged, they threatened, the guard was turned out, and finally the King himself appeared and asked what it was all about. But at that moment the sun rose, and there were no brothers to be seen – though away over the place flew eleven white swans.

And now the whole populace came pouring out of the city gate, eager to see the witch burnt. A poor broken-down horse pulled the cart in which she sat. She had been given a smock made of coarse sacking; her beautiful long hair hung loose about her shapely head, her cheeks were pale as death, and her lips moved slightly as her fingers kept weaving the green flax. Even on the road to her death she would not give up the work she had begun. The ten shirts of mail lay at her feet; and now she was doing the eleventh, while the mob jeered at her.

"Look at the witch – the way she's mumbling! No hymn-book for her, no, it's her loathsome black magic she has got there. Take it away from her, tear it into a thousand pieces!"

And they all crowded in on her to tear up what she had made. But eleven white swans came flying down and perched around her on the cart, flapping their great wings till the crowd gave way in panic.

"A sign from heaven! She must be innocent!" many of them whispered, though they didn't dare to say it aloud.

The executioner then seized her by the hand – but she quickly threw the eleven shirts over the swans and, lo and behold, there stood eleven handsome princes! But the youngest had a swan's wing instead of one arm, for his shirt had a sleeve missing, which, she hadn't had time to finish.

"Now I may speak," she said. "I am innocent."

And the people, seeing what had happened, bowed down to her as to a saint; but Elise herself, after all the strain and fear and suffering she had been through, sank back lifeless into the arms of her brothers.

"Yes, innocent she is," cried the eldest brother. And then he told them all that had happened; and, while he was speaking, a perfume as of a million roses spread around, because every faggot from the stake had taken root and put out branches, and a high sweetsmelling hedge stood there with crimson roses. Right at the top was a single flower of the purest white, glittering like a star. This the King broke off and laid on Elise's breast, and she awoke with peace and happiness in her heart.

And the church bells all rang out of their own accord, and huge flocks of birds came flying in. The bridal procession back to the palace – no King had ever seen the like of it before.